GAME FACE

JOHN WAYNE COMUNALE

Co-Published by
Awesome Dude 4 Life Press and Avantpop Publishing

Copyright © 2025 by John Wayne Comunale

First Edition

The story included in this publication is a work of fiction.
Names, characters, entities, places and incidents are
products of the author's imagination or are used fictitiously.
Any resemblance to actual events or locales or persons,
living or dead, is entirely coincidental.

Without limiting the rights under copyright reserved above,
no part of this publication may be reproduced, stored in or
introduced into a retrieval system, or transmitted, in any
form, or by any means (electronic, mechanical,
photocopying, recording, or otherwise), without the prior
written permission of both the copyright owner and the
above publisher of this book.

Cover Design by John Wayne Comunale
johnwayneisdead.com

Avantpop Publishing
avantpopbooks.com

To the countless hours of my youth lost to watching this stupid shit.

1

BLAKE PULLED AT HIS TIE with one hand and turned the knob on the door to his apartment with the other. His Uncle Gene was the one who taught him how to tie a tie and seeing how he was coming home from the man's funeral; the connection wasn't lost on him. A slight chill ran down his spine as a tinge of misplaced and unnecessary guilt crept across his psyche. While it shouldn't bother him, he felt slightly disrespectful unknotting the tie he learned to wear from a man whose body was freshly covered with dirt.

Rather than taking it off completely, Blake only loosened it some leaving the knot intact. It was a compromise he didn't have to make but felt he should. He hated dressing up or wearing anything that wasn't a t-shirt and jeans, and while he could take the tie off anytime, his uncle would be dead forever. Keeping it on a little longer was a small concession to pay somewhat of a tribute to the man in his own way.

This wasn't the first family member Blake had lost in his life, he'd also endured the death of some close friends over the last few years. These were people his age who weren't supposed to die in their youthful prime but had been scurried off into that goodnight prematurely, nonetheless.

Jason had the car wreck that took his fiancé out with him, both were hammered drunk. Tina's cousin, who only visited during the summer, died at the start of the year from cancer she'd barely been diagnosed with a month prior. Richard's suicide came just three weeks after that, but he was more of a work friend, and the incidents were unrelated.

Those deaths were hard and scarier than most as they hit in a way that forced Blake to face his own fragile mortality, but losing Uncle Gene was taking a far greater toll on him.

Blake threw his keys on the kitchen counter and headed for the refrigerator from which he plucked a cold bottle of beer before making his way to the couch in the living room. His apartment was small, and all of this was accomplished in a dozen steps or so. The fatigue incurred over the last several days made it feel like a slog. Uncle Gene was his mother's brother, and the frantic tearful call Blake received from her in the middle of the night announcing the death was tattooed on his brain.

Blake's sleep had been light and fitful since. He was unable to shake the anxiety that surged through his system whenever his head hit the pillow. Having to deal with his mother's already legendarily explosive benders on top of the flaming alcohol-fueled grief-dumpster she'd become zapped every ounce of available strength in his system.

It was an odd thing, his uncle's death, and the details surrounding it were still muddied and unclear, but Blake hoped now that the funeral was over, things would be cleared up. Though the death seemed odd to his mother and him, it wasn't being investigated or even considered as possible foul play. It came out of nowhere, which is what anyone will tell you about death. Blake's mother insisted her brother was exhibiting strange behavior and having cryptic conversations with her in the days leading to his death, but her judgment and perception of time were known to be chemically compromised.

'Strange behavior' and 'cryptic conversations' best described Uncle Gene on any given day, so he didn't lend much credence to either of those things being clues as to what put his uncle into, what Blake considered, an early grave.

Blake kicked off his dress shoes as he sat on the couch, some cheap black leather loafers he found in a discount bin, then put his feet up on the coffee table.

He took a long drink from the cold bottle as he reached for the small wooden box perched on the armrest of the couch. From it, he removed one of several joints along with a lighter that lived in the box as well. Blake rested the beer between his legs, took the joint in his lips, and pulled hard as he fired it up filling his lungs with as much smoke as possible. He exhaled a massive cloud of dankness and already felt relaxed before the last of it escaped his lungs. The smoke hung above his head in the small room vanishing slowly one whisp at a time, until the only evidence of its existence was solely aromatic.

He took another hit and placed the joint in the ashtray on the table exchanging it for the remote control. Blake sat back on the sofa, took another drink, and turned on the television. He already knew what he wanted to watch and punched in the numbers for the *Game Show Channel* before taking the joint back from the ashtray.

A classic episode of *Match Game* was on. It wasn't what he was hoping for. He left it and smoked his joint. Blake zoned out on Charles Nelson Reilly's smiling face as the beloved actor spun another double-entendre of an answer to a vaguely suggestive question, neither of which Blake actually heard. The cadence of the back and forth told him all he needed to know, and the enthusiastic response of the studio audience proved the joke was well received.

He was fond of game shows, but it was Uncle Gene who'd been passionate about them, *and* the only reason Blake watched them to begin with. Uncle Gene was a quirky man with specific tastes and interests. Ever the confirmed bachelor he remained single. Blake remembered when he was younger his uncle brought different male and female 'friends' to Thanksgiving dinner a few years in a row.

He never brought the same person twice, and while he appeared to enjoy the accompaniment, the man was never as loose or comfortable as when he was by himself. By the time Blake was twelve his uncle stopped bringing 'friends' to family functions and holiday get-togethers, which happened to coincide with the ramping-up of Blake's mother's alcoholism. It was also when the two bonded over Uncle Gene's affinity for game shows, which went beyond watching them on television. Uncle Gene had been attending different game shows as a studio audience member for Blake's entire life and many years prior.

Instead of watching the parade or football games that year, his uncle found a channel playing old game show reruns. This was before there was a network dedicated to airing them twenty-four/seven, so finding a block of classic syndicated gems running for a few hours on a random station was a treat. An episode of *Let's Make a Deal* was a few minutes in, and Monty Hall was currently speaking with a couple dressed as chickens who responded with excited squawks.

A smile crept across his uncle's face flat and tight, a quivering purse like he was trying to suppress the expression but not hide it completely. Blake thought it was because of the chicken people until he followed his uncle's sightline and saw he was looking past them, behind the main action of a deal being made. Once he realized what he was looking at, Blake opened his mouth to speak but could only point instead.

Sitting in the audience smiling and emphatically clapping along was a much younger Uncle Gene.

"Hey," Blake said finally. "Is . . . is that you?"

His uncle's smile broke open and he giggled. Blake had heard him laugh before, but this was different. This was a childlike titter subtly laced with mischievous undertones like he'd suddenly become a cartoon villain. Uncle Gene slapped his knee and nodded.

"That it is," he said. "That it is."

The young Uncle Gene on the screen wasn't dressed in a silly costume like everyone around him nor was he wearing one of the token oversized nametags. His participation was in attendance alone.

Blake's uncle wasn't someone who wanted to be *on* the game shows, but rather he enjoyed being *at* them. His uncle never tried to solve puzzles or blurt out answers as he watched to best the contestants or showoff his mental prowess. He loved every aspect of what went in to making a game show and was enamored by the entire package coming together to fire on all cylinders. Uncle Gene wasn't one to criticize, despite there being objectively more bad game shows than good. His uncle took them for what they were admiring the effort if nothing else.

Now years later, Blake hoped to turn on the *Game Show Channel* and catch a glimpse of his uncle in the audience, a sort of final nod and wave from beyond the grave. While Uncle Gene had been in attendance for many tapings of *Match Game* throughout the different eras of its run, this was not one of them.

Most of the appearances he was able to catch were stored on Blake's DVR, but his uncle had shelves of video cassette tapes on which he'd captured himself. Nowadays, the episodes could be found on the internet with minimal effort, but Blake liked the idea of having something that belonged to him even if it was a digital recording on a box he 'technically' rented from the cable company.

Blake took another hearty hit of the joint and left it to smolder in the ashtray while finishing off his beer. He let the empty bottle sit between his legs and rested his head back as the euphoric high snaked its sizzling comfort up the back of his legs, along his spine, and into his head.

***

Blake opened his eyes and sat upright to find the *Game Show Channel* still on, only now a late-era version of *Family Feud* featuring Steve Harvey as host played serving as the only light in the room. He didn't know how long he'd been out, but the lack of sun told him several hours had passed. He took his feet off the table and upon touching the floor an explosion of pins and needles rendered his appendages temporarily useless.

Blake gritted his teeth against the discomfort and moved the empty bottle from between his legs placing it next to the ashtray. He stamped his feet and rubbed the back of his calves attempting to hasten the recovery succeeding only in exacerbating the uncomfortable sensation.

If he hadn't looked up in that instance, he'd have missed it for sure. The camera had just cut from Steve Harvey to a sweeping shot across the small set of bleachers where the studio audience clapped because a lit sign instructed them to do so.

All were enthusiastically participating in the act of obedience save for one lone dissenter. The person did not smile or clap. They stared in the camera, eyes darting around as if searching for something within the lens.

The glimpse was brief, and the shot was in constant motion, but Blake recognized the puzzled straight face in the crowd. It was Uncle Gene. He grabbed clumsily for the remote with both hands intending to rewind and pause for confirmation but instead accidentally turned the television off. Darkness swallowed the small space. Blake cursed as he fumbled with the remote dropping it once before being able to turn the T.V. back on. A commercial for Cheerios appeared and the chance to rewind was gone thanks to his button blunder.

While having the confirmation would've been nice, Blake knew that was his uncle in the audience. The quick glimpse didn't result in the rush of happiness he anticipated, but rather inspired a sudden intense dread.

Uncle Gene had been in attendance for many *Family Feud* episodes, but was a staunch Richard Dawson man, and while it pained him to do so, vowed he'd never be in the audience again after the host was replaced. Blake thought it had more to do with there now not being a chance for his uncle to receive one of the famous Dawson kisses. Uncle Gene neither confirmed nor denied his nephew's suspicion.

On top of that, it appeared to be a recent episode, but the version of Uncle Gene he saw was from at least a decade prior if not more. It was not how his uncle appeared in the last years of his life, but it *was* his uncle.

Blake hoped he was wrong, and the weed had been good enough to give him visual hallucinations. He even hoped he'd dreamt the whole thing but had to be sure. He dug the cellphone from his pocket and called his mother not realizing it was after three am.

2

THE CALL WENT ON FOR A WHILE despite the late hour but provided no information. Blake's mother was not only awake, she'd been power-drinking since the service that afternoon and was making little sense.

"Are you sure? I mean, he always told me after Dawson left, he never went back."

Blake was scouring the guide on his television searching for a rebroadcast of *Family Feud* episode, but so far coming up short. He could see where the program aired each day at the same time, but no additional information was attached. There was only a title and general description reading: *Families team up against families in this classic game show.*

The sentence could literally be used to describe ninety percent of the channel's content and offered no delineation between episodes. This meant searching for it on the web could take a few minutes or a dozen lifetimes depending on what keywords you used.

Blake's mom was the only other source of information on the matter, as she was typically knowledgeable of Uncle Gene's appearances and proclivities surrounding the choices he made regarding them, but per usual she'd consumed a weekend shore leave's worth of liquor in twelve hours. Her reliability and credibility were *always* questionable regardless of her state of mind. Despite achieving this dazzling level of intoxication the woman swore she knew what she was talking about.

"Oh honey," she mumbled slurring her words. "Your uncle went to so many game shows not even he could keep track of them all."

It wasn't true as Blake knew his uncle kept very close track of the shows he'd attended. He kept a written record in a moleskin journal, but also seemed to have a computerized breakdown in his head that he could access and cross-reference at any time. What she was saying didn't sound right. Uncle Gene had been getting older and was stubborn at times. It was possible his memory had been slipping, but his pride wouldn't let him admit it.

"Yeah, I know," Blake replied. "I remember him being pretty adamant about this though like it was a sticking point for him. I don't know mom, it was strange. The guy I saw didn't just look like Uncle Gene; it was him. I would say I'm ninety-eight percent sure."

"So maybe it was," she said. "Maybe it wasn't. What difference does it make? We're all upset. Maybe you saw Uncle Gene because you've been thinking about him so much over the last few days your brain . . . tricked you."

"Yeah mom . . . I'm sure you're probably right." Blake was frustrated with the conversation and ready to get off the phone. "It was such a recent episode though, I mean . . ."

"Blake, oh my Blake, I miss him too." His mother had begun to bawl again. "I want to talk about what happened to him. Something's not right I'm telling you. Something is not right, and I intend to—"

"Okay mom, sounds good. I think you're breaking up. I can't hear you. Get some rest, and I'll call in the morning. Bye."

Blake ended the call before she could say something to convince him to stay on the line, then held his breath waiting for her to call back. When she didn't, he exhaled, threw the phone on the cushion next to him, searching through the guide on the television again. Finding the same useless non-information, Blake had the idea to check the station's web page thinking it may provide more detailed descriptions of their programming. Only it didn't. In fact, the official website offered less in the way of info as it listed only the name of the programs minus the generic description provided by the digital guide.

"Fuck it," Blake said to himself as he stood.

It was close to five in the morning now and he'd decided to call it quits on his search. After some real sleep he'd take another look with fresh eyes and a clear head. For all he knew, he'd imagined seeing his uncle and would realize as much when he woke up. Blake stumbled through the small apartment to his bedroom and finally pulled the tie completely loose before unbuttoning his shirt.

He let both articles fall to the floor while undoing his pants and stepping out of them. In the morning he'd roll them in a ball and deposit it on the floor in his closet. There it would stay until the next life event requiring he wear professional attire cropped up. He crawled into bed, twisted the sheet around him tight like a second skin, and was out when his head hit the pillow. However, his sleep was not peaceful.

Nightmares about Uncle Gene started the moment he closed his eyes until he opened them again. In the dreams, Blake saw his uncle in the audience of game shows watching from the camera's point of view without the buffer of a television screen. He was stuck within the machinations of the camera itself unable to escape its confines. He saw his uncle in every audience that panned across the eye of his nightmare. Though there were many different versions of Uncle Gene each one was experiencing various forms of inexplicable horror.

One Uncle Gene was screaming and waving emphatically trying to get Blake's attention only no sound came out of him. He appeared to be stuck to his chair, but a moment later Blake realized it was because he had no legs. His torso had been fused to the seat. In another audience his uncle purposely avoided looking into the camera to the extent his head made a full three-hundred-and-sixty-degree rotation revealing he had no face. No matter what angle Blake's camera eye looked he could only see the back of his uncle's head.

There was another audience comprised of nothing but his uncle. Every seat in every row was taken by a different version of Uncle Gene, and not just age-wise. Some of the variants appeared to be of an alien species while others were odd hybrid creatures with clawed and tentacled appendages. Despite the mashup, each was inexplicably recognizable as Blake's uncle.

One eerie instance included an audience filled with a version of his uncle when he was at the end of his life. Only in the dream, he seemed somehow older than Blake remembered him looking before he died. They were withered and sad looking, not at all like his uncle was in reality. They sat stone-still and silent staring at something just outside of Blake's view.

Just before Blake woke up, he saw his uncle sitting alone in an otherwise empty studio audience. Uncle Gene sat dead-center while the rest of the bleachers burned around him with an angry heat. He didn't try to escape or call for help. Uncle Gene sat in his seat as the fire grew closer and laughed. Actually, he giggled. It was the same giggle he made when they saw him in the audience of *Match Game* all those Thanksgivings ago.

Blake could hear the maddening cadence of it ring through his head and quickly decay as he opened his eyes and sat up in bed. He was sweating as if he'd been sitting in actual burning bleachers, and his sheet-cocoon clung to his damp skin. He peeled away the moist sheet and got out of bed nearly tripping on his discarded pants before taking his first step.

His mouth was dry, and he was hungry, but first he needed to piss. Blake took his phone from the nightstand on his way to the bathroom and saw it was just after 2 pm. He imagined his mother was still sleeping off her grief-bender or he'd otherwise be looking at countless missed calls from the woman, of which there were none. In fact, he had no missed correspondences from any friends or family save for a single spam email.

Blake pointed his dick at the toilet while navigating to open the message and saw it was an ad for, ironically or coincidentally, the *Game Show Channel*. He went to delete it out of habit but stopped short when the words *Family Feud* caught his eye. The information the ad provided was as vague and basic as the descriptions he'd read the night before. Beneath a smiling image of Steve Harvey, it said: *Family Feud. Every day at 2:25 am. Don't Miss It!*

While it was odd to advertise a show coming on at that hour, Blake knew in the age of cell phones and voice activated assistants, it wasn't all that strange. He'd been searching *and* talking about *Family Feud* on his phone mere hours prior and was watching the show on his television at that time. It only made sense for targeted ads like this to show up throughout the day. He'd be more surprised if they didn't.

His gaze lingered on the words *Don't Miss It.* The implied sentiment felt personal like it was meant for him only or . . . especially. The message seemed important, like disobedience came with weighty consequences.

Don't. Miss. It.

He wouldn't either. Blake didn't know exactly why he felt so compelled or why it seemed so important, but he would absolutely *not* miss the 2:25 am airing of *Family Feud*. With a flick of his thumb the email was deleted, then he tucked his dick away, and went about starting his day despite it already being well into the afternoon. He brushed his teeth and went over the events of the evening in his head contemplating the validity of it all.

In the light of day, his memory seemed hazy and doubt-filled regarding his sighting of Uncle Gene. He was starting to feel a little silly about the whole thing. His mother, while hammered when they spoke, had a point and was most likely right. Blake had been thinking nonstop about his uncle for the last several days since his passing, and the funeral served as a sort of system overload to his brain.

He was surprised he hadn't seen Uncle Gene in *every* audience on television and even chuckled at the thought, although his laughter died when he remembered his nightmares. He'd all but forgotten on his walk from bed to the toilet as they dissipated into the fog lifting from his waking brain. Now though, Blake could see with terrifying clarity as if he were looking at photographs in an album.

It wasn't just images of odd scary versions of his uncle forcing their way through his recall, there was also the giggling. His uncle's childish titter would typically bring a smile to his face but now the lilting laughter launched like a phantom from the back of his mind bringing with it images of the man burning alive in the bleachers. The giggling haunted him through his shower, and he dressed quickly hoping the laughter would stay in the bathroom when he left.

It followed Blake to the kitchen making him sick to his stomach, so he pulled out his phone, and paired it with the Bluetooth speaker by the sink. He started a playlist consisting of *Sleep, High on Fire, Electric Wizard* and a random smattering of similar artists hoping the drone of detuned guitars and warm fuzzy bass licks would cleanse the palette of his mind.

The music plodded along like a brontosaurus through a thousand-mile swamp, as Blake started a pot of coffee and stared into a mostly empty refrigerator. He absently looked over at the clock on the stove seeing it was close to 3 pm now, and in less than twelve hours he'd be parked in front of his television to watch *Family Feud*. He would, 'not miss it'.

Blake had no idea why he felt so compelled to do so or why it seemed so important. His memory wasn't great, and all the pot he smoked didn't help. Lately, he found himself forgetting what he was talking about in the middle of a sentence at times. Any other day he would've forgotten about the email advertising the show seconds after seeing it, but now he commanded perfect recall over the message. It was clearer in his memory than the faces of most people he knew.

Though the information was powerfully important to him, the thought was gone a moment later. Blake sipped his first cup of coffee and was on to thinking about how he'd spend the rest of what was left of his final day off for bereavement. In the morning he'd have to get up at a decent time and head in with the rest of the schlubs at the call center where he worked. Blake briefly wondered if any of his coworkers watched *Family Feud* but decided he didn't care on the way from the kitchen to the couch. He took the half-smoked joint from the ashtray, put it to his lips, and cared even less. He almost forgot about his 2:25 am date with Steve Harvey. Almost, but not completely.

The rest of the day passed quickly and inconsequentially consisting of Blake getting stoned on the couch and napping on and off. He got up sometime around dusk to make a sandwich, which he ate in three large bites then promptly fell back to sleep. Blake woke with a start, three hours later, confused and disoriented until he realized he was still on the couch in his living room. He thought he'd felt something rouse him like a slap to the face or an electric shock. Suddenly it didn't matter what woke him up, and he frantically grabbed his cellphone from the coffee table to check the time.

Blake knocked over the ashtray in his haste spilling a healthy amount of ash along with several roaches across the living room floor. He found his phone and the remote control at the same time as they were next to each other, (had he left them that way before falling asleep?) and stared into the dimly lit screen finding it was 2:23 am. He was just in time to watch his show.

His show?

It seemed odd to refer to it like that in his mind since he'd never been an avid watcher of *Family Feud*. Blake watched a lot of game shows with Uncle Gene and still never considered any of them one of *his* shows. If it were *The Simpsons* or even an old episode of *Married... with Children* it would make more sense calling it his show, but for whatever reason in this moment *Family Feud* carried just as much weight with him as either of those programs.

Blake held the remote in his other hand and turned on the television already tuned to the *Game Show Channel*. He didn't remember doing so before he dozed off after eating his sandwich, and in fact thought he remembered watching *Prom Night 2* while halfway paying attention between reading gossip articles on his phone. Blake figured he must've changed the channel before falling asleep to be ready for when the show, *his show*, came on.

Had he even turned off the television before his nap? He struggled to remember but when the familiar theme song kicked in, he didn't care, and his entire focus shot like a laser toward the program. He wasn't watching for the questions, joke answers, the *real* answers or even Steve Harvey's famous mugs to the camera. For him, they were just filler between quick shots of the studio audience.

Blake had no interest in the game. He was looking for Uncle Gene, and it didn't take long to find him. When the family introductions were wrapping up, the camera cut to the audience laughing at a hacky Harvey quip. Toward the top right in the last row of bleachers sat the same version of Uncle Gene he'd seen the night before, younger than he was when he died but not by much, and he was not laughing.

His lack of mirth wasn't the only reason the man stuck out from the brainless knee-slappers surrounding him. It happened quick, so fast Blake nearly missed it, but he'd been ready this time, or ready for *something* at least. He'd been keeping a tight hold on the remote with his fingers positioned over the correct buttons this time and was able to pause the program at just the right moment.

It was faint, but clear enough for Blake to know he wasn't imagining what he was seeing. Frozen in the frame on screen was his Uncle Gene wearing a pensive expression, his eyes looking far to the right like a child giving a last look over his shoulder for an authority figure before plunging his hand in the cookie jar.

There was no cookie jar, but his uncle was holding his hand up, palm facing the camera. In real time he'd flashed it quickly as if giving a small wave to the camera, but the still image showed there was more to the fleeting gesture. Very clearly written on the palm of his uncle's hand were the words 'help me'.

3

"I KNOW MOM, YOU SAID IT a hundred times already." The last half hour of the conversation had been exhausting. "You keep saying you thought something was strange about Uncle Gene's death, but you haven't told me any specifics. What exactly was so 'strange' about it?"

"Well, it was just so sudden, you know th—"

"Yes mom, yes I do," Blake interrupted. "*Because* you told me several times."

"When they took him away, they didn't let me see the body, you know."

That was something he *didn't* know. He was surprised she hadn't said it already, led with it even, but at least he was getting somewhere. He let her continue.

"Already had him zipped up in a bag by the time I got to his apartment," his mother said after a beat as if expecting to be interrupted again. "They whisked him right past me into the ambulance and slammed the doors before I knew what was happening. They were two blocks away before a police officer told me your uncle was inside."

"But," Blake started. "You saw the body at the hospital though, right? Or at the morgue or wherever they put bodies. You had to identify him, right?"

The following pause lasted too long.

"*Right* mom," he said again. "You saw the body, didn't you?"

"Well, no. At least no one asked me if I wanted to. They just told me he was dead and that was that. I didn't figure they needed me for anything else or they'd have said something. I didn't want to see him like that, you know . . . dead. I wanted to remember him the way he was without that image of him lying on a slab forever tainting my memory."

Blake didn't call his mother to stoke the flames of fear or add to the possibility of there being any sort of conspiracy behind his uncle's death. He hoped she would snuff out those ideas with logic and facts; he'd even take a classic mom answer of *just because*. He could accept *just because*, but not what she was currently telling him.

"Mom," Blake tried hard to reign in his exasperation. "I know the last week has been hard and a lot has been going on, but I need you to think and try to remember if you actually saw Uncle Gene's body before it was cremated."

"No," she said almost immediately without taking the time to think as Blake advised. "No, I told you I didn't want to see him dead. I signed some papers and that was that. A day later they called to say his ashes were placed in an urn and sent to the funeral home for the service. Why are you asking me these things?"

He could hear the crack in her voice and knew she was getting upset, which was not his intention. He also heard the unmistakable clatter of the cap coming off a vodka bottle and the tinkling of ice in a glass. Blake didn't tell her he'd seen his uncle again on *Family Feud*, or that he seemed to be signaling for help. He mainly wanted to poke around for information that would help him talk himself out of thinking what he saw was real.

The show remained paused; a still image of the cryptic message written on his uncle's hand was frozen on the television screen. Blake had taken several photos with his phone but trying to photograph something on a T.V. screen was as effective as attempting to snap a picture of Bigfoot. You can tell something is there, but it's always grainy, blurry. Never in focus.

In the pictures the man looked nothing like his uncle, and the message on his hand was completely washed out. Still, he hoped he could do something to sharpen the image or make it even slightly clearer. He couldn't keep his television paused forever, and in his post-nap haste had forgotten to record the show so turning it off would mean losing the image for good, or until he could find a rerun of the episode.

"I'm sorry mom." Blake was staring at his blurry and distressed looking uncle on the screen. "I'm not trying to upset you. I'm just . . . uh, having a hard time too, you know. I loved Uncle Gene, and I guess I'm . . . I just want to make sure he wa—"

"Dead? Is that what this is all about? You think because I didn't actually see my brother's body that he's not really dead? Do you think I'm stupid, Blake? Why would y—"

"No, no, no mom," he interrupted. "I was saying I wanted to make sure he was being treated respectfully in death, that's all. Like, I didn't know Uncle Gene wanted to be cremated."

His mother went quiet again, the pause lasted too long for Blake's comfort.

"I guess I didn't either," his mother finally said. "I figured he had it all worked out with, well; whoever it is who handles those things. Your uncle was always particular *and* prepared, you know."

Now it was Blake's turn for a long pause. He'd called his mother to be comforted and convinced he was making too much out of what he'd seen but so far felt like maybe he wasn't making enough out of the odd Uncle Gene sighting. The things his mother was telling him left all sorts of doors open for conspiracy and conjecture, though he dared not bring it up to her.

"Mom," Blake finally said. "Has anyone gone inside Uncle Gene's apartment since they took him out in that bag?"

4

BLAKE SENT AN EMAIL TO HIS SUPERVISOR when he got off the phone with his mother saying he'd be taking an additional day off. He'd have to use sick time to cover it, but he had plenty saved up and tried not to think about the work stacking up on his desk. He could always go in on Saturday or stay late the rest of the week, which was a small tradeoff for the peace of mind he'd get from finding Uncle Gene's apartment free of anything suspicious.

The sun was starting to rise when Blake stepped out of his own apartment hoping it was still early enough to beat traffic on his crosstown drive. He double checked to make sure the spare key to his uncle's apartment was still on his keychain. He had the key from when he was supposed to water the plants while Uncle Gene was on a vacation to somewhere he couldn't remember. It was years ago, and he hoped the locks hadn't been changed in the meantime. If so, he'd have to make a trip to his mother's place for a new key, a hassle he'd like to avoid.

He made good time and arrived relatively quickly to the building. He even found a prime parking spot right in front of the door. It was easy, but the kind of easy that felt wrong. Like he was getting away with something at someone else's expense. Blake decided to get a coffee from the cafe on the corner before going upstairs. He was hoping the walk would help calm his nerves and clear his head but only gave him more time to dwell.

When he approached his uncle's apartment, coffee in one hand and key in the other, nothing looked abnormal from the outside. He didn't think it would be roped off in crime scene tape or boarded up with 'No Trespassing' signs but thought there'd be something . . . different. Something to indicate a death had taken place. Like a wreath or skull or even a cross on the door. Something . . .

Blake paused and wondered if police and first responders had to have the landlord open the door, or if it was left unlocked. He tried the knob and found a key wouldn't be necessary after all as it turned in his hand. Before he pushed the door opened, he tried to remember if his mother told him who exactly called the paramedics. Was someone with Uncle Gene or had something occurred to alert people on the outside he needed help?

Maybe it was Uncle Gene himself who called for help as he was experiencing . . . what exactly? Heart attack? Stroke? Blake assumed one or the other was responsible for taking his uncle's life despite the man having been in good health but was now realizing he had no idea. Grief had filled in the blanks in his mind as he reeled from the initial shock. He was struggling to make sense of something he hadn't wanted to accept.

The outside of the apartment may have been free from damage and blemishes but as the door swung slowly open, Blake saw the same couldn't be said about inside. His instinct was to step back and check the door again hoping he'd accidentally entered the wrong apartment, but no matter how badly he wanted it to be a mistake, he knew he was in the right place. Only a version where things had gone terribly wrong.

The first thing Blake noticed, what drew his attention instantly, was the television or lack thereof. The seventy-inch behemoth was missing from its place of prominence on the far wall facing the entrance to the apartment. Uncle Gene had lived in the same place for as long as Blake had been alive. While the television itself changed sizes, brands, and cable packages throughout the years, its placement was always the same. It not being there felt wrong. It was like he was staring into an open chest cavity from which the heart had been savagely wrenched.

Another thing he noticed right away was the smell. His Uncle Gene's apartment never had a smell before, unlike most domiciles Blake visited that weren't his own. Some places smelled like the ever-lingering spices of frequently prepared foods, while others smelled like the occupant's pets and their accompanying menagerie of aromas. His mother's apartment smelled of potpourri and rose perfume. One of Blake's friends once described his apartment as smelling of weed, old beer, and older beer. None of which were offensive to him.

Uncle Gene had no pets, wasn't much of a cook, and did not smoke weed or anything else in his apartment. Still, there was a definite lingering odor Blake couldn't put his finger on. Like burnt electricity without the smokiness that comes when a physical object is on fire. He thought he'd heard a coworker refer to this type of smell as 'ozone' although Blake wasn't sure what that meant exactly or what could be the cause.

He slowly edged his way through the door into the narrow entryway with his head on a swivel unsure what he was looking for. Blake closed the door behind him, and his ears popped like he'd been sealed in a pressurized cabin prepping for space travel. The uncomfortable pressure in his head aside, the apartment was completely still. Not just quiet but vacuum silent. He cleared his throat to make sure he could still hear and hadn't gone suddenly deaf.

It was only a few steps from the entryway to the living room. Blake took them slowly, his eyes darting madly around the room as he entered searching for anything else amiss. He made it to the couch and stepped over to the window, which was unlocked as well, and he raised it several inches. He told himself it was to air out the electrical smell, but he really wanted to let some of the city sounds in. Hearing the cars, breeze, and occasional obscenities lobbed back and forth from frustrated commuters made Blake feel like he wasn't completely cut off from the outside world or trapped in a capsule hurdling through space.

Blake looked back at the blank spot where the television had been realizing he may very well be in the middle of a crime scene that hadn't been investigated because no one knew there was reason to, yet. He turned back to the window and used the bottom of his t-shirt to wipe away any fingerprints he might've left behind, which was easier than having to try and explain to a detective why they were there. He was a relative after all, but that only meant he'd be amongst the first investigated if foul play was determined as the cause of his uncle's death.

Blake wondered if he should call the police right then to report the television was missing, he knew that much for sure, but thought better as he pulled his phone from his pocket. He wanted to look around more before jumping to any conclusions. He'd circle back with his mother later to see if she happened to know anything about the missing T.V. Also, he doubted the police would consider something stolen from the apartment of a dead man high priority.

From where Blake stood in the living room the rest of the apartment appeared in order, immaculately so, as his uncle was known to keep a neat and tidy place. He wasn't an overbearing clean freak with a complex but curated a certain esthetic which included an element of organization.

Blake put his hands in his pockets to avoid the temptation of touching anything else and stepped carefully to the bedroom. He looked inside, moving his head just past the door frame and saw everything was in place. The bed was made, and the drawers were all closed, which cast doubt on his robbery theory since the apartment hadn't been tossed. If a robbery occurred, especially if it happened in the days following his uncle's death, they would've rummaged through everything and left a mess.

Blake crossed to the kitchen, went to flip on the light, but caught himself before touching the switch. There was enough light coming from the living room window for him to easily see what was on the counter. It was a television remote control. There was no reason for it to be sitting next to the sink since the T.V. couldn't be seen from the kitchen. As far as Blake knew it served no secondary function requiring such placement.

When he got closer, he could see something was wrong with it and used the flashlight on his phone to get a better look. A divot had been melted into the smooth plastic casing surrounding the red rubber 'power' button like the last thumb to press it had been on fire. The edges around the indentation were singed and crumbly, and small black flakes of plastic dotted the counter on either side of the remote like frozen dead ants.

Blake grabbed a towel hanging from the handle of the oven, used it to open a cabinet above the sink, and then removed a plastic sandwich bag from a box within. Using his limited police investigation knowledge, all of which was based on reruns of *Law & Order* and *Forensic Files*, he turned the baggie inside out to use it like a glove to pick up the remote from the counter. He pulled the plastic up and around before sealing it in the bag so as not to touch it with his bare hands.

He stepped out into the light of the living room to take a better look and found the remote dotted with sticky brown splotches that clung to the inside of the plastic bag. Blake thought the substance was maybe cooking grease but on closer inspection it appeared to hold a more sinister quality. He couldn't say for sure it was blood, but that was his first thought. It could very well be a mixture of sweat and grime, no reason for him to jump to conclusions although no amount of sweat would cause that kind of damage to the device.

Uncle Gene had been in decent shape before he passed but wasn't one to work out strenuously. He went for daily walks which as far as Blake knew were short and low impact. Even if he'd upped his regiment and started pushing himself harder shortly before he died, he would have to have been sweating up a storm while handling some form of filth before using the remote.

Blake shoved the baggie in his back pocket and paced behind the couch in the living room. He walked to the window and looked down at the sidewalk hoping something would spark some inspiration, but his mind remained blank, so he resumed pacing. He didn't know what to do next and wasn't sure if he was making a big deal over nothing. The only thing missing in the apartment as far as he could tell was the television, and if whoever took it stole anything else it wasn't readily apparent. He couldn't imagine the world's most fastidious and tidy thieves just so happened to rob his dead uncle's apartment then cleaned up after themselves before making off with the goods.

A thought occurred to Blake that maybe the television had been taken by the paramedics or even the police. He'd heard stories of first responders keeping cash and jewelry they found on people who were either dead on arrival or sure to expire before making it to the hospital. He liked to think it was something that didn't happen often or was mostly a rumor, but the world didn't work like that, not anymore. Everyone was out for themselves and stealing from the dead, while far from honorable, was easy pickings.

Blake looked to the empty space where the large television had been mounted and noticed something on the wooden stand just beneath. The piece of furniture had served as the television's home before the time of flat screens and wall mounts. The few drawers on the front held extra linens, Christmas ornaments, and various sundry like loose batteries and a myriad of cables belonging to different electronics. Since the television went to the wall, his uncle hadn't kept anything on top of the stand. No lamp, framed family photos, or decorative knick knacks.

He kept it clear and dust free, which was why it made no sense for there to be a VHS tape sitting atop the otherwise clear surface. More unnerving was Blake didn't recall seeing it upon his initial inspection. It was possible he'd been distracted, the large empty space on the wall usurping his attention directing it away from small details. Blake told himself as much as he approached the television stand though wasn't entirely convinced, but considering an alternate theory was too much to process in the moment.

He stepped around the couch refusing to take his eyes off the tape for fear it would vanish then stared down at it for several moments. It was in a generic white cardboard sleeve with the brand name, MIRIM, situated at an angle across the front in red letters. Not one he remembered, but there were countless generic brands. His uncle and mother bought blank tapes in bundles of three or five, but that was years ago, and he couldn't remember the last time he'd seen one.

The antiquated form of media was out of place sitting on the old T.V. stand because it didn't belong there, but also because his uncle didn't own a VCR. He knew this because Uncle Gene had given it to Blake's mother with a box of old tapes years ago during Christmas. He'd embraced digital technology and saw no reason to keep the items when a hard drive in his television could record his shows, and streaming allowed him to watch movies anytime he pleased.

Blake reached out and gently lifted the tape handling it as if it might crumble to dust in his hands. He wasn't worried about leaving fingerprints because he already knew he was taking the tape with him. Handing it over to the cops would all but guarantee he'd never get to see it for himself. He'd watch it first and determine if it contained anything useful but doubted it would.

He turned the tape over in his hands and on the spine written in his uncle's unmistakable handwriting it said: *Game Face*. It looked like Blake would be making a trip to his mother's place after all.

5

 it was the one that should be investigated. The esthetic of her décor bore earmarks of a classic breaking and entering, though the state of disarray was not caused by an intruder. These were the ever-present results of her waxing and waning perma-bender, and Blake doubted she'd slept more than three hours at a time since receiving the call about Uncle Gene.

He'd seen her go off like this before when his dad left and again when she was laid-off from the bank, but he was much younger then, and it was never this bad. It was possible he never realized how truly bad it was. His uncle did a good job of shielding Blake by distracting him with game shows in hopes of creating some good memories around the sinking ship of a life his mother was captaining.

"Mom? Hey mom." Blake pushed the door open, having used his copy of her key to let himself in when she didn't respond to his knocking. "Mom, it's me. You awake?"

He stepped over her winter coat, which was on the floor in the entryway rather than hanging in the closet where it belonged, and accidentally kicked over one of three empty vodka bottles pushed up against the wall. It clattered loudly across the tile down the hall and continued rolling through the living room where it was stopped by a random pile of towels. They'd most likely been dumped there to cover up a spill, or vomit, or both.

Next to the towels were two empty wine bottles, one upright and the other lying on its side. A few feet away Blake found more towels and a case worth of empty champagne bottles situated around them like traffic cones marking off a construction zone. The smell of booze overpowered the potpourri, though whiffs of rose perfume lingered adding a unique underlying foulness to the sour aroma. He wondered if he should be more concerned about his mother. She was still alive after all, and until he found reason to believe otherwise his uncle was dead.

"Mom?"

Blake called again hoping he hadn't jumped to conclusions by assuming his mother was alive. There were a lot of empty bottles lying around, and she was never all that nimble. There were countless ways for her to have fallen in the living room alone, but so far there was no sign of her.

"Blake? Blakey honey, is that you?"

The sound of his mother's voice from the kitchen gave him a start, though the immediate rush of relief snuffed out his annoyance. He hated when she called him Blakey but seeing as it meant she wasn't in the shower with a broken neck, he'd let it slide.

"Yeah mom," he answered, making his way to the kitchen. "It's me. I was calling but you—"

Blake stepped into the kitchen and stopped short. He wondered briefly if he'd been wrong and what he was seeing was indeed *not* preferable to finding his mother in the shower with a broken neck. Dishes were stacked high in the sink stuck together by full servings of food stuffed between like cream in an Oreo. There was nothing appealing about this particular filling though, no compulsion was sparked to lick the tasty treat from between plates. He could smell the food-turned-adhesive rotting from where he stood at the entrance of the kitchen. Fruit flies and gnats swarmed in a small gray cloud around the sides of the stack while larger black blowflies landed on the lumpy piles of slush at the top.

His mother sat at the kitchen table with her legs up on the chair across from her lounging back and smoking a cigarette. She was wearing a white satin robe that had fallen off her right shoulder exposing half a breast from which Blake quickly averted his eyes.

"Jesus Christ mom," he said snatching a dish towel from the counter and throwing it at her. "Cover yourself up. What is going on in here?"

Atop the table was a jumbled mess of food leftover from the funeral competing for space with a smattering of vodka bottles. Some less full than others. There were cakes and assorted pastries, but most of the real estate was taken by casseroles, a meatloaf, and two lasagnas, one being vegetarian.

All of it had been left out unrefrigerated since she'd brought it home.

Blake's mother gave a chuckle, waved the towel away, and pulled her robe back into place while straightening up in her chair. She gestured at the seat her feet had been in for him to sit down.

"You want some coffee? You'll have to make some. I haven't gotten around to it yet."

She had a coffee cup sitting in front of her next to an ashtray overflowing with the grim remains from a multitude of *Virginia Slims*. Blake could see the liquid in the cup was not coffee, a notion confirmed when his mother reached for the vodka bottle closest to her and topped it off.

"No coffee for me mom," he said choosing to remain standing. "Maybe you could use a pot yourself . . . or two. What is all this? This place is a mess, like a *bad* mess. I know you miss Uncle Gene, I really do get it, but this?"

Blake gestured around the room while his mom nodded sipping heavy from the mug. He swatted a fly buzzing around his head and moved away from the bio-hazard incubating in the sink. He went to grab the trash can from the other side of the fridge intent on beginning the disposal process but found it already overflowing, the lid lying next to it on the floor.

"I know Blakey, I know," she started. "And I was feeling better earlier, I really was, and I'd even started picking up the place."

She gestured to a seemingly empty garbage bag under the table indicating she hadn't gotten very far.

"So, what happened?"

"Well, after I talked to you, and you asked me all those questions I didn't know the answer to, I . . . I didn't know what to think anymore, I guess. I felt . . . dumb for not making sure I saw the body or going to his apartment. Then I stopped to sit and think about the night Gene died, and I guess I haven't gotten up since. I thought I remembered something too, but then I don't know. I think I was trying so hard to remember I forgot."

Blake's mother raised her mug as if making a toast then downed the rest of the vodka it held. He winced from the tinge of guilt he felt at unintentionally causing her to spiral and second guess herself while trying to force memories into existence that may have never happened. He decided not to tell her about his trip to Uncle

Gene's apartment so as not to induce further mental anguish. He just needed to borrow the VCR. She didn't need to know the reason.

She went to grab the bottle for a refill, but Blake beat her to it, sat in the chair next to her, and poured her the drink. He held up the bottle and toasted her back before taking a swig from what was left.

"Mom," he started. "I didn't mean to make you . . . feel bad. I was just curious and maybe I sounded harsher than I meant. I . . . uh, can I borrow the VCR?"

6

AS BADLY AS HE WANTED TO TAKE THE VCR and go, Blake couldn't leave his mother's apartment in its current state. The clean-up took longer than it should've because she kept interrupting to babble drunkenly about how sorry she was until thankfully passing out on the couch. Blake filled five trash bags with empty bottles and spoiled food and did his best to rinse the plates well enough to be put in the dishwasher. Most of them were too far gone to clean, so he left them in a sink full of soapy water to be dealt with later.

He used his foot to move all the dirty towels into one pile in a corner not wanting to touch them with his hands, then hung up his mother's coat and the few other clothing items he found scattered about. The stench of old food and cigarettes mixed with perfume was thick and cloying, so he opened the windows in the living room and kitchen. The smell had been locked inside long enough to attach itself to the drapes and furniture. It would take some time for the apartment to air out completely.

After a bit of searching, he found the VCR at the bottom of the hall closet beneath a stack of old board games and a box of pint glasses he'd left there years ago when he moved out. Blake had a habit of stealing them from bars for a while but abandoned his precious collection when the reality of having to *actually* move everything he owned came into play. He'd thrown away an impressive collection of crap he'd once held dear in the span of three hours while questioning what his attachment was to it to begin with. His mother insisted he donate the glasses, but the box never made it out of the closet.

Blake could only carry three trash bags down with the VCR tucked under his arm, so he decided to leave the remaining two beside the door in lieu of making trips. He was afraid his mother would wake up and suck him back into a guilt-laden, never-ending, circular conversation for another hour. It was already getting close to noon, and he didn't want to waste any more time.

When he got to his car, Blake checked the center console where he'd stashed the remote and the video tape. There was no reason for them not to be there but seeing them gave him an odd sense of comfort. The VCR sat on the passenger seat for the ride home, which he again made in record time despite anticipating hitting lunch traffic. If the circumstances were different, he'd be able to enjoy what was shaping up to be the best luck he'd had driving in the city ever. Unfortunately, that wasn't the case.

He had to dig through a few drawers in his desk but eventually Blake found an adapter to connect the VCR to a television never intended to accept a signal from such a prehistoric device. Once it was set up, and he'd slid the videotape inside the machine, he sat on the couch looking from the VCR to the melted remote in his hand for another twenty minutes.

He'd removed the remote from the bag when he'd first gotten home to take a closer look under decent light. Blake did his best not to touch the sticky splotches but no longer cared about leaving his fingerprints. Absently, he rubbed his thumb back and forth across the melted divot while working up the nerve to start the tape.

He debated smoking a joint first but decided he'd keep his head clear just in case. Blake didn't want what he was about to see clouded with doubt from an altered state of mind. He'd have to go into this clean and sober then move toward intoxication depending on what he found.

Blake bent forward to reach the VCR reminding himself it could be nothing both figuratively and literally. The tape could very well be blank or filled with old sitcom reruns of no consequence, but the atmosphere in the apartment took on a sudden sinisterness the moment he pushed play. It was like the air had been chased from the room, and the stale, uncomfortable, stillness left behind bristled and scraped the exposed skin on the back of his neck.

He'd made sure the tape was rewound, but it began in the middle of a program like the recording had been started late. The sound was muffled, and the image was fuzzy but eventually both issues were resolved after the first thirty seconds.

It was an episode of *The $10,000 Pyramid* Blake pegged as being from somewhere in the mid-seventies based on the look of host, Dick Clark, and the celebrity guest to whom he was currently speaking, Tony Randall. Uncle Gene loved this and all subsequent versions of *The Pyramid* game show that followed. He'd been in the audience more than a few times though not until the mid-eighties and wouldn't be popping up in this one. Or at least he shouldn't. The image of his uncle from *Family Feud* came to his mind prompting him to keep his eyes peeled.

The clock had just begun to countdown the current round between Tony and the non-celebrity contestant he'd been paired with, an unfortunately humble looking woman with a dead tooth and deader eyes. The game started with one team member being given seven words having to do with a mystery category. That person then gives clues to their partner using any form of 'verbal communication' while they try to guess the words. The teammate giving the clues must be careful not to accidentally say the word or another form of it, but otherwise most anything goes.

Randall was trying to give clues describing the word on the small screen in front of him, each attempt being met with a gaping mouth and shrugging shoulders. The words were displayed at the bottom of the screen for the viewers at home to see, and Blake gasped audibly when the first one appeared.

It said *Uncle*.

Blake held his breath as Tony Randall passed when it became clear his partner wasn't getting it, and the next word came up.

Alive.

Randall fired off a list of clues, none of which his partner seemed capable of understanding let alone able to discern from his spot-on context clues. Flustered but keeping a smile on his face, Tony passed to the next word.

Trapped.

Blake breathed deeply now trying to maintain a slow even pace and keep from hyperventilating. Randall's partner kept shaking her head like a mechanism in her neck was malfunctioning, and he passed on to the next word rolling his eyes when it came across his own monitor.

Mistake.

"Come on Dick," he joked with the host. "I mean . . . come on."

"The clock is ticking!" Dick Clark laughed through a mouthful of teeth bigger than his face.

Time was running out and rather than even try, Randall passed immediately.

Please.

Tony passed.

Come.

He passed again, and when the final word appeared Blake was hit with a disorienting sense of déjà vu.

Help.

The buzzer sounded, and Tony Randall threw up his hands in a comedically oversized gesture of frustration. Ever the consummate professional, he smiled through the whole ordeal while his partner laughed and clapped idiotically with ignorant enthusiasm.

The last thing Blake remembered before blacking out was Dick Clark revealing the category the words were supposed to be describing.

Hostage.

7

BLAKE KNEW HE WAS DREAMING. He was sure of it, which didn't make the experience any less terrifying. Uncle Gene was in an episode of *The $10,000 Pyramid*, not as a member of the audience but as a contestant. He found himself sitting on stage at the familiar round table across from Tony Randall who was looking down at a small monitor in front of him. The situation was nearly identical to what he'd watched on the videotape with him in place of the mouth-breathing Midwestern mother.

Dick Clark glowered over the space between them bearing teeth that went from his chin to his forehead. He was saying 'the clock is ticking' over and over without moving his lips like a recording was playing somewhere behind the wall of white chompers his face had become. Instead of lobbing clues between quips, Tony Randall continued to say only 'pass' without even trying. His level of aggravation was noticeably ratcheting up, but he made no attempt to tamp it down with humor now. He was angry plain and simple and didn't care who knew it.

Blake tried to calm the man and coax him into attempting the game, but he was unable to speak. The host seemed only capable of smiling while shrugging his shoulders. Tony passed again and again having gone way beyond the usual seven clues. He snarled when he said the word and frothed at the mouth while Dick Clark's maniacal laughter echoed from behind a freakish mammoth smile.

Tony Randall threw his hands up. A rage-filled, garbled cry erupted from his throat as a warning to anyone within earshot to get as far away from the sound as possible. Blake couldn't get away though because he not only couldn't talk but couldn't move. He didn't seem to have any control whatsoever over the form he inhabited in this scenario. Blake could only watch the crazed actor in front of him rip the monitor from the table, stand to his feet, and lift it over his head. Dick Clark's teeth brushed against the stage lights dangling from the ceiling, vibrating with roaring guffaws.

Tony Randall continued wailing incoherent babble showering Blake's face in spit a moment before slamming the monitor down on his head. Everything went black for only a moment like he'd blinked. When he opened his eyes, Blake found he was still on the show but now watching from the audience. The people around him roared, heaving exaggerated bursts of laughter from mouths too big for faces on which eyes were situated too close together.

Blake had a clear view of the stage from his new vantage point and saw Tony Randall using the monitor to beat the person at the table across from him. Half a second ago that person had been him, but now Blake watched from the safety of the audience while someone else took his beating.

"It's a shame." The person sitting next to Blake spoke into his ear to be heard over the laughing and screaming. "He can't take too many more of those."

"More of what?"

Blake turned and saw the person speaking to him was a younger version of his Uncle Gene. Before he could react, the man answered.

"The beatings," he said, pointing at the stage. "Those goddamn beatings."

Blake looked back toward the action and realized the person being pummeled by Mr. Randall was also his Uncle Gene appearing as he had shortly before his supposed death. Blake looked back to find the person next to him was now one of the big-mouthed, small-eyed, Luddite laughers. The Uncle Gene on stage sat still and took his lumps without trying to move or fight back. He didn't call out for help or go unconscious. He just sat smiling as the monitor came down across his head over and over.

Each strike inflicted another layer of damage to Gene's already ravaged visage. His left eye was swollen shut, and the side of his face became a lumpy purple mush as his skull collapsed inward under the fervorous blows. It was like the dream where he watched his uncle sit and giggle while burning alive. This time everyone was laughing except Uncle Gene.

Bits of broken teeth fell from his mouth dotting puddles of blood on the table with sharp shards of pointy white and yellow pebbles. Hair stuck to the monitor and dangling scraps of scalp hung like slippery streamers clinging for dear life to fractured follicles. Dick Clark's teeth nearly eclipsed the stage as Uncle Gene's right eye ruptured and drooped loose from the broken socket, dripping, empty, and useless.

Finally shaking the shock from his system, Blake stood to scream for Tony Randall to stop beating his uncle, but as he did the scene dropped out of frame and everything went black again. This time Blake's eyes were open. It didn't seem like he'd changed positions as he had earlier, but rather everyone else had.

It wasn't completely dark either. Most of the space around him was black, but there were random patches of flickering light that moved like electrified scratches across the darkness. They flashed in and out growing then shrinking amorphously as he watched. The crackling frantic light looked close enough to touch, but reaching out you'd find it was much too far away.

"Careful, those can really sting."

Blake recognized the voice behind him and reeled around to face the version of his uncle who'd been sitting in the audience next to him seconds earlier.

"What?"

"Those scratchy-looking flickering lines are the 'tracking'. They're sharp as hell. Electrified too." Uncle Gene explained.

"Where am I?" Blake mustered.

"I could explain, but there's not much time on the videotape between shows," Uncle Gene said. "This is actually one of the few blank spots left and it doesn't last long so listen up."

"Blank spots? What are you talking about? This is a dream." Blake was trying to convince himself. "It is, isn't it? A dream?"

"No, my dear nephew it is not." The image of his uncle flickered and blurred for a moment as he spoke. "You're not in a *dream*, but you are in the *tape*. Well, sort of. At least that's the best way to put it."

"What am I do—"

"I'm getting there, just let me finish," his uncle interrupted. "I told you we don't have a lot of time. You're here to save me. Well, *him*, but it's me too. Mostly."

"Save you from what? You're . . . you're right here. That, or you're really dead. You're supposed to be, at least."

"You're half right. Like I said, by me I mean him. The uncle you saw on stage taking a walloping from ol' Felix Unger over there."

"Felix who? I thought it was Tony Randall?"

"Never mind. He's the version of your uncle who needs saving. I exist regardless."

"But what are you?"

A high-pitched whine sounded from off in the distance and his uncle's expression went deathly serious.

"I'm from the original recording but that's been recorded over many times. Now I exist like a phantom in the background only seen in random small glimpses, but even then; I'm barely visible."

The whine was getting louder making it hard for Blake to concentrate. He kept thinking the sound was coming from outside his dream, and he'd be waking up any second now realizing he'd left the tea kettle on. Only he didn't drink tea, and he wasn't waking up.

"Are you trying to say I'm . . ." Blake paused, unsure of how to ask the question. "I'm *in* the videotape? Is that what you're telling me?"

"Yes! Yes, you are." This version of his uncle was

excited, but maintained a stoic tone. "So is your uncle, the one who's not me. The one you need to save. He's in here and now so are you. If you don't get to him before the tape ends . . ."

"Tape ends? Like I'm on a timer or something?"

The whine sound was right on top of them now as the area around became slowly brighter like the sun was rising. The man standing in front of him started to flicker and fade.

"That is exactly right," the younger version of his uncle said, his face blurring. "He survives the first show because it starts in the middle. They didn't have enough time to take him out completely, but the rest of the tape will be a crapshoot."

"So . . . so what are you saying? What do I do?"

"You have to make sure your uncle survives. Get to him, and then you both need to find a way out of here. Like I said, you only have until the tape ends to figure it out."

"What? How do I even—"

"They're coming."

The image of his uncle flickered then fizzled out completely before the world around Blake suddenly lit up with music blaring down from above.

8

IF BLAKE WERE PLAYING *Name That Tune*, he would've nailed the song in two notes, maybe three. The scratches in the darkness, the 'tracking' as he'd been told, were chased away by the colors and flashing lights of a game show he was perhaps the most familiar with, but only because it had been on for so long. In the background, he heard an omniscient announcer cue the audience who then screamed in unison the words, *Wheel! of! Fortune!* Blake realized he was yelling right along with them.

The scene stabilized and he found himself in the first row of the audience with an unobstructed view of the familiar colorful wheel, the contestants, and the seemingly ageless Vanna White who manned a wall of squares ready to turn them and reveal the letters behind when guessed correctly. It was the familiar setup Blake had seen through the years on his own television set as even his mother was an avid 'Wheel Watcher'. Some things were strangely off from how he remembered the program, though.

Blake scanned the contestants finding none of them to be his uncle and then noticed the wheel. Rather than labels featuring dollar amounts, prizes, and pitfalls, the spinning offerings available were replaced with acts of violence. Unsavory objects were attached to some spaces like a large, half rotted, dead fish while others had different weapons affixed to them. There was a machete, a medieval looking sword of some kind, and a small hatchet with hair stuck to sticky splotches of dried blood. Another odd macabre offering included a severed hand Blake hoped was a prop but knew it wasn't.

Longtime host of the popular game show, Pat Sajak, didn't seem to be himself either. His smile was exaggerated like Dick Clark's had been, but rather than extending up to take over his face, it stretched around to the back of his head with the sides nearly touching. His hair was styled up and back in an overly large pompadour reaching two feet from his scalp and looked to be made of modeling clay. Black eyeless slits were situated in his head releasing random puffs of smoke that hung around the highest portion of Pat's hair like fog on a mountaintop.

Upon closer inspection of Vanna, she didn't appear the way he remembered the bombshell co-host looking on the television screen. Vanna's signature blond hair was still intact, but it writhed and squirmed atop her head like a separate sentient entity. Her smile was big, white, and while larger than normal it wasn't as grotesquely overdone as Pat and Dick's were.

Yet, there was something off about it. Blake had to squint to see her teeth were smaller versions of the light-up tiles she was there to turn over. Across the top row it said *FUCK*, while the bottom read *OFF*. Blake noticed when she removed her hands from her hips, they wriggled in undulous waves, as fleshy serpents with fangs embedded in her fingers.

Blake took this all in while attempting to process what he'd been told moments earlier by the disappearing version of his uncle. He didn't understand why this was happening or what exactly was causing it, but he knew what he was seeing and feeling. If Blake was here to save his uncle, his *real* uncle, then where was he in *this* scenario? The three contestants situated around the morbid wheel were versions of a psychotic and twisted reality themselves, but Uncle Gene was not among them.

Blake turned in his seat scanning the audience. At the very top left side of the bleachers, he saw his Uncle Gene smiling and clapping along as the show got underway. He waved to try and catch his uncle's attention, but the man didn't *or* couldn't see him. His anxiety surged when he looked back to the stage as the game began. The first contestant was a uni-browed man with a gut the size of a small boulder his already over-taxed t-shirt failed to contain. The protrusion matched the hump on his back in size and shape. He spun the wheel with an appendage that was more flipper than hand, ferociously clapping like he was trying to bring Tinker Bell back to life.

The wheel stopped on the space with a machete attached, which must've been a good thing because the contestant clapped and yelped in excitement.

"Okay shit stick," Pat Sajak said to the contestant. "What's your letter?"

"Z," the man said, still clapping his pseudo-flippered hands like mad.

"Let's see Z, Vanna."

The woman's smile never faltered as she shook her head and shrugged, the serpentine arms roiling and churning to create a sickening effect.

"Oh, looks like there's no Z, shit stick," the host said.

Pat Sajak reached forward, plucked the machete from the wheel, reeled back, and buried it in the man's neck. The contestant honestly didn't seem surprised by the brutal act and even managed a smile and half-hearted flipper wave to the camera as a crimson geyser spewed from the wound spattering the wheel below. The blood spray quickly weakened to short, small bursts, as his heart slowed and became a trickle. The man finally collapsed forward smacking his head against the wheel then sliding backwards to the floor. A chunk of bloody scalp dangled from one of the pegs attached to the wheel.

The audience around him exploded in applause with some even standing and whooping in elation.

Blake stood as well looking back to check if his uncle was still at the top before making his move. Blake shot out to the aisle a few seats away stepping over and on the mindless bovine-people making his way up the steps. Behind him, he heard the show continue as the next contestant was prompted to spin the wheel.

Blake had only taken two steps before it became hard for him to move, which he realized was because his feet were sticking to the floor. He grabbed the railing trying to pull himself loose but was stuck tight.

"Uncle Gene, it's me Blake! Hey! Uncle Gene!"

Blake shouted and waved his hands, but his voice was drowned out by the applause around him. Thinking quick, he bent down, untied his shoes, and stepped out of them. Rather than putting his socked foot back on the flypaper stairs, Blake turned and stepped directly into the lap of the man sitting in the aisle seat. He felt their genitals squish between his toes, but instead of crying out in pain the man looked, smiled, and grabbed Blake's ass.

Blake panicked, stepping lively across laps and legs hurdling his way to the top row through and over one delighted masochist at a time, all seemingly exhilarated by his ball-crushing escape. He was halfway up the bleachers when there was a change in crowd. Their collective attention turned to what Blake first thought was him until he paused to look over his shoulder. Pulling himself over the railing and into the first row was the host himself, Pat Sajak, wielding the machete he'd since liberated from the first contestant's neck.

"Where you headed, friend?" Pat called up to Blake, his voice a gravel-filled saccharine waterfall. "Don't you want to spin the wheel?"

Pat brought the blade down into the head of the woman Blake had been sitting next to causing the entire audience, including her, to whoop in delight. Her blood was a bright neon arc of electricity that soared through the air lighting up everyone it touched in the audience. Pat put his foot on the side of her head and yanked the blade free sending a red lightning storm of castoff across the stage behind him.

The host wasted no time stepping over seats to come after Blake chopping and hacking at overly enthusiastic audience members along the way as if he was clearing a path through the jungle.

"Shit!" Blake yelled, and climbed faster using tops of people's heads for balance before pushing off to propel himself forward, hastening his momentum. He made it a few more rows before audience members grabbed hold of his arms and legs trying to slow his ascent as Sajak closed the gap between them.

"Uncle Gene!" He screamed while beating back the clawed and slimy hands grabbing for him but didn't dare stop to take a closer look. "It's your nephew Blake! Help!"

The irony of asking for help from the person he was supposed to be rescuing wasn't lost on him, but he couldn't get his footing, and Sajak was close behind. His uncle's joyful expression turned puzzled as he looked at Blake with absolutely no recognition in his eyes.

Pat was a row away and had the machete pulled back ready to swing down on his head, but Blake yanked his foot free from the slick grip of his captor, clamoring up another row, and out of the way of the host's range at the last second. The blade came down into the large belly of the man who'd been holding his leg. From the wound spilled out a gushing sea of ruptured intestines sending a tidal wave of squirming guts rushing down the bleachers.

"Looks like he should've bought a vowel," the host yelled, yanking the machete from the man's ruptured stomach.

The audience ripped into applause again, but Blake didn't dare stop to look back. He kept his eyes on his uncle as he clamored up the remaining few rows separating them. Uncle Gene stood realizing the action was heading right for him and seemed genuinely frightened which only confused Blake. For a man who was supposed to be in trouble and needed rescuing, Uncle Gene didn't seem so happy to see the cavalry coming. In fact, his uncle was now pushing himself back against the railing trying to put a few more inches of distance between him and his would-be savior.

Blake stepped over the final row of seats. His foot came down on someone's slimy secretion, and he slipped under the railing and off the top of the bleachers just as Sajak swung the machete, narrowly missing his head.

"Shit, shit, shit, shit, shit, shi--, ooof!"

Blake yelled as he fell and hit the floor landing hard on his ass. He looked up and saw the host glaring down, his doughy surrealist features fixed in a hate-filled sneer while shaking the machete over his head like a British nanny with a problem child. Blake struggled to catch his breath and saw Sajak turn his cyclone of violence in Uncle Gene's direction.

"N--, ugh. No!" Blake coughed the words willing his diaphragm to loosen its hold around his lungs. "Stop!"

The host paused and turned to look down again as Blake managed to prop himself up on his elbows. Sajak extended the arm the machete was not attached to and shot him the finger. When he turned back to slice Uncle Gene, Pat slipped in the same slick of mystery discharge and tumbled over the railing as well. Blake rolled out of the way and used the back of the bleachers to pull himself up as the host landed face first on the cold concrete floor with a wet smack.

The audience went quiet and still while Sajak lay motionless. Blake clung to the bleachers catching his breath, but the stillness didn't last long. A moment later, the crazed host's crumpled form began to vibrate. He picked his head up and thrust the machete, which he'd somehow kept hold of, wildly in Blake's direction. The crowd erupted with glee, stomping their feet along with their raucous applause.

The host struggled to get to his feet and Blake looked up just in time to see three audience members, one being his uncle, hoisting the body of the gutted man up and over the railing. He leaned out of the way and the body landed between him and Pat bursting apart like a ruined wet pinata upon impact. Rubbery globs of the man's mangled insides sprayed in unrecognizable chunks from the gaping wound in his stomach like someone slinging Jell-O in a cafeteria food fight. Blake pursed his mouth shut but that didn't stop him from tasting the viscera that splashed across his lips.

Sajak, finally on his feet, appeared unharmed aside from his nose being flattened against his face with the fall having somehow relocated his left eye up into his forehead. Blake caught another break when the host stepped in gooey innards and fell face down into the wound he'd moments ago been responsible for creating in the man's torso. He pulled his head up and out, and Blake saw not only was there fire in his one good eye, but the teeth of his wraparound smile had gone long and pointy.

Sajak pushed himself up and brought the machete down into the corpse's neck, severing the head in one final act of violent desecration. Blake was already making his way around the bleachers back to the stage; the pursuing footfalls fast approaching despite the incessant cheering from above.

"Come on Blake! I thought you wanted to be a wheel watcher?" Bursted Sajak.

Blake turned the corner only to run directly into the slithering open arms of Vanna White. Despite her slight petite frame, he might as well have run into a concrete barrier. There was no give upon impact with what felt like solid stone. His breath was once again knocked out of him, as her long powerful arms wrapped around his body, holding it tight against her own.

Struggling caused her grip to somehow tighten, so he stopped and tried to go slack but had no luck with that method either. He could do nothing but hang from her grasp attempting to force tiny gulps of oxygen into his constricted airways, while the otherworldly grotesque Pat Sajak hobbled toward him with a machete at the ready.

"Well, well, well, Vanna," Pat said as a pointy cylindrical tongue darted from between his teeth, swiping moisture across his top lip. "It looks like someone wants to solve the puzzle."

Blake felt the sick swell in his stomach as the host was speaking, a reflex he couldn't stop or delay. Sajak brought the machete over his head preparing to strike the killing blow, and Blake could hold it no longer. Vomit muscled its way through passages compromised by Vanna's bearhug and was ejected into the host's face. The ralph-runoff slid down his own chin onto Ms. White's serpentine arms.

Her grip loosened slightly and with the help of his lubricating barf Blake slipped through her grasp. The machete blade came down with force striking Vanna instead. It sliced across the front of her face bifurcating her features continuing down through her overlong snake arms severing them from her body at the double-jointed elbow.

Sajak screamed through a face full of puke clearly frustrated with this mishap. Chunks of her wiggling arms landed in Blake's lap shaking like massive serpent-inspired dildos. Blake looked up and saw her glaring down, the skin having fallen from her face revealing shiny emerald scales beneath. A forked tongue darted in and out of her newly fanged maw.

"Jesus Christ!" Blake slapped at the seizing limbs while scrambling to his feet. "Fuck every single bit of this shit."

The audience proved they loved what was happening through their ghoulish jubilation. They screamed, clapped, and stomped with pleasure for the entertainment they were receiving. Blake came around the front of the bleachers looking up into the crowd for his uncle, and the audience started to explode. Literally.

He saw the first one go up like a frog with a firecracker up its ass four rows from the front. She was slight and thin but had a head big enough for two of her bodies. He'd only caught a glimpse before she blew so there was a chance her noggin had inflated before detonating. It wasn't the kind of explosion you get from gunpowder being involved but rather pressure like an overfilled balloon. The sound was a muted wet pop against the cacophony of asinine applause. There was nothing subtle about the mess that followed.

A waterfall of blood and internal fluids sluiced down off the front of the bleachers soaking Blake's socked feet in organ juice. He leaned back and looked up in time to see the next audience member explode from extreme jubilation, only this one was much closer. The man was in the front row wearing cargo shorts, sandals with white socks pulled up to his knees, and a t-shirt that said *Franks and Beans Make Me Mean*, struggling against his ample girth to remain in one piece.

The audience member was already plenty swollen and exploded out from the side of his stomach like he'd been popped by a pin, only without leaving a pin-sized hole. Instead, an opening the size of the first woman's head expelled a multicolored slurry of shredded innards coating the person next to him in a dappling of gore.

A horror-filled scream came from his left. Blake looked over to see the battered, vomit-streaked, blood-soaked host barreling around the corner barreling right for him. In one hand Sajak still held the trusty machete while from the other swung one of Vanna's severed squirming snake arms. The host whipped the rubbery appendage at Blake who dodged and leaned for the stairs leading back up to the bleachers.

Blake stepped lively keeping to the edge of each step so as not to get stuck again while disgustingly plump glazed tourists exploded around him like he was navigating a morbid minefield. His uncle was still up there though, and he had to get to him. Four steps from the top, Blake realized his socks were gone. The last few sticky stairs had been ripping flesh from the pads of his feet with each step, but he was too keyed up to feel any pain.

"Blake?"

He heard his uncle cry out from the railing where he'd helped throw the gutted man over. Uncle Gene waved his arms motioning for Blake to go back, but Madman Sajak was hot on his tail hacking and slicing random audience members while others exploded in a deluge of soupy, human-stew, sludge.

"Uncle Gene," Blake called, pushing forward. "I'm here to rescue you. Stay there and I'll—"

A man jumped in his way blocking the path to his uncle. Blake shoved him into railing where he flipped over and explodes before hitting the ground, like a water balloon full of blood and shit. The blade-wielding host reached the top row and slammed the machete against the railing as he ran toward Blake sending up a shower of sparks. Blake was within feet of his uncle, reached out to take him in his arms, but was unsure of what to do.

"No, Blake. No," Uncle Gene shouted, holding his arms out to stop his nephew from colliding into him. "Not here. This isn't the rig—"

Uncle Gene exploded before finishing his sentence blinding Blake with wet hunks of decimated dermis attached to wiggling rubbery flecks of moist flesh. The force blew Blake back into the arms of Pat Sajak sending them both over the railing in a tangled mess of bloody limbs and bits of jiggly jagged tissue.

9

BLAKE BUCKED, STRUGGLING TO detangle himself from the psychotic Sajak but the slick coating made it impossible to find purchase. He braced himself to hit the floor hoping he was positioned for the host to break his fall. When impact didn't come, Blake opened his eyes and found himself no longer grappling with the machete-wielding maniac, game show host, nor was he smattered in a slurry of human juices.

Blake was surrounded by semi-darkness broken up by the random scratches of light like where he'd spoken to the version of his uncle who was attempting to provide some guidance and instruction. He looked around hoping the man would appear again to provide information Blake could *actually* use to further his . . . what? Quest? Mission? Blake had no idea what this was?

The reprieve didn't last long enough to allow for interaction even if his strange guide had appeared. Blake now found himself smack dab in the middle of another familiar game show. He was onstage this time staring at a man he recognized standing behind the host podium as Peter Tomarken. This meant the show he was in now was *Press Your Luck*. Tomarken got the gig after semi-successfully managing to shed the scandalous stink of hosting a *Playboy TV* show prior to landing this job.

Press Your Luck had become one of Blake's reluctant favorites. He remembered it took him a bit to warm up to the show since as a kid all he wanted to see were the cartoon Whammy characters. These were little devil-like animated creatures responsible for taking a contestant's winnings forcing them to start back at zero. Blake didn't initially grasp the gambling aspect of the game, and the questions that started each round were a puzzling mix of pop-culture facts from before his time. After watching a six episode mini-marathon with his uncle, staying with him during one of his mother's more destructive benders, four of which Uncle Gene was in the audience for, Blake found he actually enjoyed the show.

Now though, he wasn't so sure. Seeing as how the last two shows he'd been thrust into went, while dealing with the idea he was supposedly hurtling through the time stamps of a decades old VHS tape, Blake wasn't optimistic. At first glance, everything appeared normal. Blake scanned the space around him before looking out into the audience frantically hoping to find his uncle. He thought maybe his rescue attempt would work better if he made a move right away rather than letting the game start to play out.

Blake didn't want to be chased around a studio by another weaponized game show host again if he could help it. His tailbone was still sore from his fall from the *Wheel of Fortune* bleachers. Aside from that he seemed otherwise uninjured, and his clothes were clean. His shoes and socks were even back on his feet. He squinted against the lights and continued searching the audience for Uncle Gene while Tomarken went over a quickie version of the rules.

"Today we have Blake here from upstate New York. He's a novice screenwriter who just recently sold his first script. Blake, congrats and welcome to the show."

The hanging silence became uncomfortable before Blake realized the host was speaking to him, only nothing the host said about him was correct. He was from LA not New York. He wasn't a screenwriter or any other kind of writer. He was just a call center office drone, and even then, he mostly just goofed off. Blake cleared his throat, then finally spoke.

"H-hi there . . . uh, Peter," he managed. "Thank you. I, uh . . . I . . ."

Now that he was looking directly at the host, Blake noticed he did indeed have some unique traits. Tomarken's smile while big and toothy was proportionate to his face, but yet it was his eyes that were the issue. Blake had heard about people smiling with their eyes before, but not in the literal sense as he was seeing it now. Peter Tomarken's eyes had been replaced with two small mouths mirroring his muggy smile.

"Okay Blake, no need to be nervous," the host said. "Good luck to you."

Tomarken moved on to introduce the next contestant while Blake stayed zoned in on the host's eye-mouths. When he realized they were where the man was speaking from, Blake couldn't look away. The two tiny mouths-for-eyes were moving in sync with what Tomarken said while his main mouth maintained an unwavering winning smile. Blake stared at them mesmerized until he heard his name again and snapped out of the trance.

"Blake? Blake, you paying attention? Are you ready to win some money?"

"Y—yes," he said flatly. "I am."

"Okay, here's our first question. Buzz in when you know the answer. Out of the three of you, which one will die at the end of this episode?"

Blake was confused as the contestant to his left quickly mashed their buzzer.

"Blake," the woman cried.

"Okay, you said Blake," the host continued. "I'm going to ask the question again to your two opponents and give two additional answers for them to choose from. Out of the three of you, which will die before the end of this episode, killed in a horrible torturous fashion?"

Blake didn't remember the host using those specific adjectives the first time he asked the question.

"Is the answer Blake, Blake, or . . . Blake?"

"I say Blake," the contestant to his right said.

"Okay that's two for Blake," Tomarkin said from both smiling eye/mouths. "And you Blake, what's your choice?"

"Who, me?" Blake replied confused. "I—"

"That's three for Blake," proclaimed the host. "And the answer to the question of who will die in an awful, horrifically painful and degrading way before the end of this episode is . . . Blake! Everyone wins a spin."

The audience broke out into applause with an unsettling enthusiasm reminiscent of what he encountered from the crowd on *Wheel of Fortune*. Blake went to stand, but found he was held to his seat by one large leather strap across his waist and another over his legs just above his knees.

"Shit, not again," he said, struggling to move.

He looked over at the contestants on either side to see if they too were bound in place. They were not. Blake did find they both had the same mouth for eyes condition as the host and guessed if he could see the faces of the audience beyond the stage lights, they too would share the affliction.

"Going somewhere, Blake?" The host asked, his face literally all smiles.

"We haven't even spun the wheel yet," the woman to his left said.

"Yeah, we have to spin," the man on his right said before screaming, *"No Whammies!* No Whammies! No Whammies!"

"Well, we've only asked one question," Tomarken said, "but what the hell. Let's skip to the spins!"

A giant wall bordered with light up squares listing prizes and dollar amounts rolled out behind Tomarken from the side of the stage. It wasn't really a physical wheel they were spinning like the last show. Squares flashed randomly and whatever it stopped on when the contestant hit their buzzer was their prize. If it stopped on a square featuring the red, devilish-looking, cartoon characters Blake loved so much in his youth, you lost everything.

Blake scanned the board and saw the prizes and dollar amounts had been replaced by symbols he didn't recognize. The esthetic broadcasted a sinister quality. Most of the spaces featured mischievous Whammies while drastically increasing the contestants' odds of losing, and as his eyes quickly looked from square to square, he finally found his uncle.

Each Whammy, while different in the implement of destruction they held varying from sword to bat to sticks of TNT, all bore the face of Uncle Gene.

The woman on his left went first and shouted 'No Whammies' out of all three of her mouths as the board lit up with electric beeps and boops sounds from the background.

"Stop!"

The woman hollered and slammed her fist down on the buzzer in front of her with enough force to break it to pieces. The one square left lit up on the board was of his uncle as a Whammy holding a giant mallet of comically large proportions, though Blake couldn't imagine anything funny happening as a result.

"Oh no, you've got a Whammy coming," Tomarken said. "And by the looks of it, I'd say it's gonna' be a doozy."

Blake remembered from watching the show that if a contestant hit a Whammy a short animation would play at the bottom of the screen depicting the mischievous creature stealing the person's money in a humorous fashion. He had a feeling it wasn't going to work that way this time and was correct.

The female contestant who'd 'hit the Whammy' didn't seem the least bit fazed or even upset. In fact, she was more enthusiastically jubilant than prior to spinning the wheel, making Blake wonder how she would've reacted had her spin stopped on one of the strange symbols. A whoosh sounded from behind and over Blake's shoulder a Whammy rose from a trapdoor in the floor behind the woman's seat.

It was dressed in a red unitard and holding a real-life facsimile of the mallet from the drawing. The audience ripped into applause whooping and whistling as the life-size Whammy came into view while Peter Tomarken laughed with three mouths. The woman continued to clap and cheer but didn't look behind her as if she already knew what was there but didn't care. The Whammy raised the hammer gripping the handle in both hands. The crowd's noise level elevated in time with the motion.

"Hey, look out," Blake called to the woman oblivious of his attempt to warn her. "Hey! Hey! Heyyyyyyyy! No!"

When the Whammy had the hammer lifted as far as his arms could go Blake caught an unobstructed view of its face. It was his Uncle Gene.

"Uncle Gene? Uncle Gene! No, wai—"

Blake's pleas were cut short as the hammer came down with thunderous force on the woman's head obliterating it in an instant. If he blinked, Blake would've missed it and wished very much he had. Though it wasn't the worst thing he'd seen on his excursion so far. The strength behind the strike was of a caliber his uncle did not possess at any time in his life, let alone in the end.

The woman's head was reduced to bloody brain sludge with bits of skull, teeth, and chunks of muscley gore spackling the side of Blake's face as they were ejected from ground zero between her shoulders. Remarkably her hands continued to clap ferociously for the first few seconds before slowly coming to a stop as if she were a child's toy whose battery had just run out.

The massive hammer's head was stuck halfway down the woman's neck hole while Uncle Gene struggled to dislodge it amidst the eruption of applause and the host's obnoxious laughter. Blake spit crunchy chunks of cranium and wrenched his head back yelling to get his uncle's attention.

"Uncle Gene, it's me! It's Blake!"

His Uncle was focused on removing his hammer, but when he finally did turn to Blake his entire face changed. The aggressive sneer fell away, and the anger lifted from his eyes as recognition set in. In that moment he finally looked like the Uncle Gene Blake knew and loved.

"Blake?" What are . . . You shouldn't be here!"

"Yeah, no shit and neither should you," Blake fired back. "I'm supposed to save you or something, I think. Either way get me out of these straps and let's get out of here."

"Oh Blake . . ." The host's voice was several octaves lower now as it boomed from the podium. "It's not a good idea to talk to a Whammy. Everyone knows that."

The audience shook the stage with their combined belly laughs like it was the funniest thing they'd ever heard. The remaining contestant on the other side of him continued screaming his chant of *No Whammies* while Blake struggled against the bonds, pleading with his uncle for help.

"Uncle Gene, please. We have to go."

"No Blake, no." Now his uncle looked genuinely terrified as he spoke. "*You* have to go. *You* have to get o—"

"I don't believe our Whammy should be talking to contestants either."

Tomarken yelled climbing over the podium hoisting himself with two additional spideresque limbs that sprouted from his torso. All three mouths dripped a green foamy discharge that hissed and sputtered as it burned through the floor where it landed. Blake pleaded with his uncle as he struggled desperately against the straps bonding him to the chair. The host crawled closer, and the acidic substance pouring from his eye/mouths as it melted the flesh on his face, contorting his features into something an amateur taffy puller might create by mistake.

Blake screamed and fitfully yanked at his bonds as the man next to him continued to yell about wanting 'no whammies'. Only now his eye/mouths had opened wide allowing thick hairy spider legs to force their way out from the confines of his skull.

"Uncle Ge—"

He turned to make one last appeal for his uncle's help as the hammer came down on his own head.

10

IT DIDN'T HURT. In fact, for the briefest of moments Blake felt the most incredibly relaxing sensation he'd ever experienced. It was like how he felt when he would mix the Vicodin he was prescribed for having his wisdom teeth out with a beer or two, only multiplied by a thousand. Blake felt so good his entire being could break apart, dissipate into the ether, and he'd be just fine with not existing any longer. If this was what dying was like, Blake would fight to come back just to die again just to re-experience the perfect weightless warmth once more.

He'd have to hold fast to the memory for the time being because the blissful sensation stopped all at once leaving a cold dreary heaviness in its place. Blake could see again finding himself in the familiar dark space as scratches of light raced past his face like echoes of lightning. Without thinking, he reached out and grazed a patch of illumination then quickly pulled his hand back. The minute amount of contact left his fingertips scorched and bleeding from what felt like touching fire with sharpened knives for flames.

"Oh shit." Blake shook his hand, then blew on his fingers while assessing the damage. "Son of a bitch, that stung. What the hell is that shit anyway?"

"I told you it's the tracking. Remember I said it *wasn't* a good idea to touch those."

The voice of Uncle Gene came from behind him, so Blake whirled around narrowly dodging another flying burst of light scratches.

"You!" Blake's voice raised. "Where the hell did you go? I thought I wa—"

"I know you're angry and confused," his uncle butted in. "Like earlier, we don't have much time. You can continue your tirade and learn nothing, or pipe down and listen while you still can."

Blake started to respond, thought better of it, and nodded instead. As badly as he wanted to have a melt-down, it wouldn't be productive. If the only way out of this horrendously hellish nightmare was to save his Uncle Gene, the *real* Uncle Gene, he could hold his tongue for now to find out how.

"Good then," Uncle Gene continued. "Your uncle has been here a while and he's . . . confused. He believes he belongs here. Thinks he's better off. He's not just going to walk into your waiting embrace so you can swing off together on a vine to safety. You need to force him to go with you and by that, I mean you're going to have to *use* force."

"But why does he need to be saved from a place he wants to be? How did he get . . . wherever we are in the first place? How the hell did I even get here?"

"Sorry, no time."

The phantom of his Uncle Gene flickered then dissolved into static as light and color quickly rolled in taking over the surrounding space Blake found himself trapped in.

11

A SEAT ROSE FROM BENEATH HIM. Blake stumbled back into it landing between two lumpy oafish men wearing neon-colored caps and overstuffed fanny-packs. They were cheering through mouthfuls of circus peanuts, spraying wet orange fluff on the backs of people in the row directly in front of them. From somewhere over their heads an enthusiastic announcer's voice boomed.

"Who's ready to play *Hollywood Squares?*"

The entire audience, now fully materialized, stood in unison, clapping at the command of a large, flashing, neon 'Applause' sign. Blake found he was standing and clapping as well but quickly caught himself and stopped. He didn't know how he'd gotten so caught up in the fanfare. Was being in this place messing with his brain? Was the tape affecting him the same it was supposedly affecting his uncle? Blake wondered if he was starting to believe he was *supposed* to be here as well.

"Circus peanut?"

The man on Bake's left nudged him offering a handful of the orange marshmallow goo spilling from the open fanny-pack. He only had one mouth located in the proper area of his face, but when he smiled Blake saw the reason the man was so keen on the soft novelty food. He had no teeth. None at all. The toothless maw was rimmed in pink and red gums peppered with weeping sores and quivering white-headed pustules. Indentions where long-ago teeth had once been, were now black and dripping thick pearls of puss-filled infection.

"N—no thanks," Blake said.

"More for me." The man continued freakishly gumming the marshmallow mess.

The man shoved his hand into his mouth up to the wrist, raking across his gums erupting several bloated boils along the way. No sooner had he removed the hand from his mouth, the other one was jammed in taking its place with another sloppy tangerine-colored handful. Blake's stomach lurched. He turned to scan the audience for his uncle once again. The wretched smell of the man's diseased mouth clung to the air around him like the lingerings of death. It was strong enough to taste.

Blake couldn't locate his uncle. He didn't have much time to look as the audience sat, and the show began. He decided to sit for the time being, telling himself doing so was entirely his idea and not due to any enigmatic influence on him. If what the young version of his uncle told him was true about having to take Uncle Gene by force, he'd need a plan. First, he wanted to put eyes on the man which was easier than expected. Blake looked up to see his uncle was smack-dab in the middle of the massive *Hollywood Squares* game board.

"Goddamnit," he muttered.

The host was actor, singer, and longtime former contestant, John Davidson, who'd manned the helm of the show during which the time period Blake had watched. It was another of Uncle Gene's favorites which quickly became one of Blake's as well.

Aside from Uncle Gene being center square, things seemed normal. Blake found himself sandwiched between two cartoonish trash people, which wasn't a far-fetched scenario according to his uncle. He'd told stories about how certain people who made being in the audience of a game show part of their vacation. Slack-jawed yokels squeezing swollen hips, cellulite-dimpled thighs, and over-distended bellies into shorts and t-shirts two sizes too small, barely able to contain the bulbous girth while collapsing under the stress of labor, like a horse needing to be shot. They were completely without shame and self-awareness, lacking in sense or the concept of an acceptable appearance. These stories made complete sense now.

Davidson already spoke to the two contestants on stage next to him, Blair and Donald, which Blake could see easily from the nameplates they wore. The host was now engaging in banter with the celebrities populating the squares. The contestants' job was fairly simple in that instead of them answering the questions, a celebrity of their choice does.

It's up to them to decide if the answer is correct or not prompting some guests to deliver long-winded, detailed, fake answers creating confusion and comedic moments, which was the true basis of the show. If they guess correctly, the square is marked with an 'x' or 'o' accordingly. The first contestant to get a tic-tac-toe is the winner.

On paper, the entire concept is simplistic and stupid, but the jokes made by the celebrity guests were what made the show a hit. Finding out the jokes were pre-written by staff writers for the show was slightly disheartening for Blake to learn when he was older. Still, he did appreciate the performative wit.

The host was speaking with the top left square occupied by the brown, hairy, alien puppet ALF. It wasn't uncommon for the program to feature that type of guest. Blake recalled previous episodes on which his favorite fluff-filled, felt-covered, hand-piloted friends from *Sesame Street* occupied squares. He remembered liking the show *ALF* when he was a kid, but the details escaped him. Though, not for long.

Watching the puppet talk back and forth with the host, he realized something wasn't right about the lovable television character from outer space. The way it moved, its gestures and inflection, its eyes. If he didn't know better, Blake would swear the creature was indeed a living entity. What happened next not only confirmed his theory, it reminded him of the show's major plot points. ALF, which stood for Alien Life Form, was an alien from a planet called Melmac. ALF crashed into the garage of some nice white family in the suburbs who then go on to have hilarious adventures trying to constantly conceal the alien's existence. All while he attempts to fix his ship and get home.

Another interesting fact about ALF was he ate cats, which was what the lifelike creature sitting in the top left square was currently doing. No, this wasn't an innocent bit between some puppet and a plush stuffed toy cat either. Blake watched as the big-eared, furry, fanged being, not of this Earth, lift a large, alive, and very real calico cat from beneath the small desk occupying the square. Davidson and the contestants chuckled while the audience around Blake cheered the alien on.

The ALF creature's mouth stretched open disgustingly wide as if his jaw was segmented like a snake's to allow adjustability according to the size of his meal. There was no need to open so wide if kittens were on the menu. The memories of ALF being a funny, lovable, relatable character were forever wiped away by what was currently unfolding.

The dilated mouth-hole revealed formerly hidden rows of sharp teeth dripping in saliva thickened by anticipation. ALF held the cat by its neck, dangling it over his feline feeding hole, gesturing with his free hand for the crowd to cheer louder. When the applause reached a decibel level acceptable to the alien, he dropped the cat into his mouth. The widened jaw snapped like a triggered beartrap returning instantly to its normal size. If the cat made any noise on the way down, it was drowned out by the insane volume of cheering that followed.

ALF gave a wave, belched loudly into his microphone, and followed it up shouting 'I kill me.' His popular catchphrase from the hit sitcom.

"Terrific," the host chuckled. "Always great to have you with us, ALF. Next let's go to . . ."

Blake tuned Davidson out, scanning the additional eight squares for other abnormalities, hoping something would spark an idea for a plan on how to extract Uncle Gene from the center square. He did worry about convincing the real Uncle Gene he needed rescuing when the time came.

The other celebrities were Sally Field, Billy Ray Cyrus, Teen-Wolf, Walt Disney's head in a jar, Crystal Gayle's hair, Skeletor, and a constantly burning brown paper bag of dog shit.

Not the caliber of guest he was used to, though nothing about what was happening made any sense. The initial sense of normalcy he'd felt moments earlier was clearly imagined. Blake accepted nothing was going to be 'normal' again until he was home. He swore once he did get back, he'd never watch another game show ever again. He might even swear off television altogether.

"And of course, we have everyone's favorite at center square today," Davidson pointed out. His mention of 'center square' pulling Blake's attention back on the host. "Mr. Gene Simmons, but you *all* know we just call him Uncle Gene. Welcome back Uncle Gene!"

The audience gave his uncle a standing ovation. Blake joined to look around for a quick and easy way to escape the seating area. He didn't understand why the host called his uncle Gene Simmons. There was no way to confuse his uncle with the fire-demon bass player of KISS. Blake wrote it off as another distraction, not allowing it to derail his train of thought. Davidson also called him Uncle Gene, leading Blake to believe they knew exactly who his uncle was and were flaunting it in his face. He didn't know exactly who *they* were, but it was clear they were now taunting him.

A sudden commotion came from the top of the game board above his uncle, cutting the conversation with Davidson short. Sally Field had used Billy Ray Cyrus's lasso to rope the country singer around his neck then pulled him over into her square, violently choking him.

"Ha! I kill me."

ALF repeated the famous line and slapped the desk in front of him before pulling another cat from beneath. Billy Ray toppled over the front of Sally's square purple and swollen from the end of the noose she'd fashioned from his lasso. At the same time, the alien's segmented jaw widened again. The audience stood whooping and cheering approval for the random chaos. Blake used the opportunity to make his move.

"Excuse me."

Blake pushed past his tubby toothless neighbor but couldn't escape making contact with sticky sections of the man's girth that left traffic-cone-colored patches of the melty mucus-like mess on his clothes. After brushing past four equally yet uniquely fowl audience members, Blake was out in the aisle and heading down the steps toward the stage floor without pausing to think.

The crowd roared with glee behind him, and he looked up to the game board to find out what evoked the reaction. Fire from the flaming bag of dog shit had crept upward toward Walt Disney's head in a jar causing the liquid within to boil. Walt's noggin bounced from side to side, screaming while scalding-hot bubbles licked scorch marks up his face.

Blake looked across the stage to see the host still laughing while the two contestants were engaged in a fierce slap fight. Their faces were red and swollen from trading of open-handed blows with neither showing any signs of slowing down. If anything, each slap was getting harder making their cheeks go raw and bloody. Blake looked back to the game board where, despite being amidst a cyclone of unmitigated chaos, Uncle Gene appeared to be genuinely enjoying himself.

Things were escalating, and Blake needed to do something now before the situation got too out of control to navigate. There'd be no need to convince his uncle to leave if he burned up in the towering inferno of the *Hollywood Squares* game board, though none of the 'celebrities' seemed concerned. He wondered if they were unaware of what was happening, or simply didn't care.

Blake raced from the steps at the base of the bleachers, past stagehands and camera operators whose backs had been to him. No one tried to stop him from running toward the fiery display. He went around to approach from the back left and immediately saw there was no saving Skeletor. Eternia's grandest villain had been reduced to a burning pile of scorched bones, his cowl and staff eradicated to dust by the heat. A similar fate befell Crystal Gayle's hair, now a charred pile of short-n-curlies that smelled like a sewage treatment plant.

The rickety wooden steps leading up to the middle and top rows of the game board had yet to be touched by the inferno. Blake raced to the stairs when he noticed Sally Field climbing down the rope that she hanged Billy Ray from, clutching a pirate-style cutlass blade between her teeth. She was shimmying toward his uncle's square. Her eyes were large, red, and segmented like a fly. Blake dashed up the steps two at a time, hoping to yank his uncle out of the space from behind before she could reach him.

"Ha, I kill me!"

Blake looked up in time to see ALF hurl a large, long-haired cat directly at him. The feline screeched a terror-riddled angry cry, becoming a fluffy ball of claws and teeth on a crash course with his face. He didn't have time to bring his hands up before smacking directly into not the freaky flying cat, but something else, something solid that he couldn't see.

Blake's ears rang from the force of impact. He shook stars from his vision, realizing right away something had changed. He was still in the same show, still attempting to climb the steps to his uncle's square, and still looking at the cat coming right for him, only now everything had stopped. Maybe 'paused' was the best way to put it. Everything around Blake was the same but slightly darker and mostly frozen in place. Mostly because the edges of everything blurred as if fighting against the invisible force holding them in place.

Blake, realizing he could still move, quickly took a step back to the side, putting himself out of the howling cat's trajectory. A patch of the familiar scratches of light shot by in bursts of tiny ugly lightning, as he looked around trying to get a hold on what was happening. The young version of his uncle called the light patterns 'tracking'. All Blake knew was he didn't want to touch it again. The cuts on his fingertips were gone, but still throbbed with a fiery phantom ache.

Something clattered behind him, and Blake spun around, nearly tripping down the only three steps he'd managed to climb. Between quivering frozen flames and blurry backstage storage items, he caught a glimpse of a face in the vibrating darkness. It was only a quick flash but undeniably recognizable as the version of Uncle Gene with whom he'd been talking. He wasn't smiling now, though. He instead wore a sinister and crazed expression. It was there and gone in an instant.

Blake looked up toward the back of his real uncle, trying to gauge how close a pseudo-frozen Sally Field was to plundering his square. While he seemed safe for the moment, everything could change with the press of a button. If Blake had to accept he'd somehow been transported to a place existing on a videotape, it only made sense someone outside of his general awareness held the power to control said tape. If the supposed 'power that be' hit play, his uncle would be mortally wounded if not decapitated completely.

The dementedly ghoulish, fly-eyed Sally Field had been stopped just short of delivering the killing blow. She was still holding onto the rope the unfortunate country star dangled from, but the sword was no longer in her mouth. It was in her hand paused mid-strike with the blade inches from gouging a trench through Uncle Gene's soft throat flesh.

Blake tried to ascend the stairs again, slowly this time with his arm held out, feeling for the invisible barrier. His fingers found the obstruction when he reached the third step, and he felt around discovering it was not confined only to the narrow staircase. It stretched out beyond the railing on both sides and went as high up as he could reach. Even from the floor, he wouldn't be able to breach the invisible force field but thought maybe he could run around the game board structure from the other direction.

He stepped off the staircase and looked back up to his uncle, shocked to see the man was moving.

He watched him pull back away from Sally Field's blade, look quickly from side to side, then dropped through the floor disappearing completely. Blake's eyes shot furiously around, searching for where his uncle had gone, but could find no trace. Uncle Gene wasn't in the square below and was certainly no longer in his own center square. He was just simply gone.

"Uncle Gene?" He said to no one. "Uncle Ge—"

Just then, Blake's ears popped, and the world around him came back to life. He'd forgotten about the incoming cat, which he narrowly managed to avoid. Its tail grazed his shoulder as it whizzed by before hitting the floor feet-first, scrambling on its claws to slow the momentum. The cat slid into the scaffolding behind the game board, righted itself, and dashed off into the depths of the backstage darkness.

"Hey, if you're not gonna eat that, could you throw it back?"

Blake looked up to see ALF waving and calling to him about returning the purring projectile.

"That's what you get for playing with your food."

Blake barely had time to admonish himself for the cornball hack comeback when a confused mutant version of Sally Field dropped from above, landing directly in front of him. The cutlass clattered, sliding across the floor, disappearing in the direction the cat escaped. The stunned actress attempted to get her footing. She bounced back incredibly fast for having hit the ground so hard. Blake realized why when he noticed the slim translucent wings protruding from her back.

All one hundred of the insect actress's eyes were pointed in his direction as she hovered a foot off the ground in front of him. She may have lost the blade, but from the looks of her teeth and hands, it didn't appear she needed it anymore. There were only four teeth visible in the small, round, tumescent mouth, and they jutted horrifically from the opening like pointed rock formations. Her long spindly fingers were curved into barbed hooks with the ends dripping thick yellow secretion.

Without hesitating to think, not typically his strong suit, Blake lunged forward, took hold of the hovering fly-woman by the wrists, and in a single motion flung her into the fire that was overtaking the three-story game board. She shrieked and spit hot vomit as she flew back into the flames where her wings burned up immediately. Sally hit the floor and skid backwards into the consuming embrace of fiery death.

With the invisible barrier gone, Blake could run to the front of the stage, the way he came, but had no idea what he'd do when he got there. He hoped to round the corner and find his uncle in the audience, possibly occupying the seat he'd abandoned earlier, but knew chances were slim. He didn't know how to get himself to the next show on the tape. It would be ideal, though, if he could make it there without being dropped, pummeled, or crushed.

He raced around the flame-engulfed game board and back through the camera operators and crew who remained silent and impassive. Ambivalent to his motives, apathetic to his existence. Blake reached the seating area but before he could look for Uncle Gene, a deafening crack sounded behind him. He whirled around to see the bottom section of the massive tic-tac-toe board had collapsed, and the second and third stories above fell forward into the laughing host and slap-fighting contestants. They kept taking turns slapping each other's faces until the moment they were crushed by the wreckage of the flaming squares.

A flock of jittery tracking patches raced across the area where the amusing structure had come apart, leaving a rift of darkness in their wake. The deafening roar of rushing air filled the studio, drowning out the constant applause of the audience.

Pieces of the flaming set, along with bodies of the crew and audience alike, were sucked through the mystical cleave in their reality. Blake turned and ducked, narrowly avoiding being smacked in the face by the railing as it ripped from the front of the bleachers and was pulled into the floating darkness.

Blake crouched, keeping low to the ground, trying to avoid the powerful suction as his circus peanut eating neighbor flew overhead dripping sticky puffs of orange marshmallow fluff along the way. Blake managed to close his mouth in time but could not avoid taking a fist-sized gooshy glob to the face.

He inadvertently stood while wiping the mess with the front of his shirt and was immediately knocked off his feet by the powerful wind. Blake was picked up in the air where he soared across the studio and into the roiling black ridge hovering above the stage.

12

EVERYTHING STOPPED WHEN BLAKE passed through the telescopic opening. The chaos of swirling smoke and fire caught in a whirlwind of debris and people was gone, like they'd been sent to a completely different place than him. Blake wasn't flying anymore. Instead, he found himself standing still in the darkness as if his momentum had been somehow negated upon the transition.

Scratches of tracking fluttered above his head and skittered along the ground past his feet, a little too close for his liking. Blake craned his neck, looking around for any sign of his Uncle Gene, either version of him, being careful not to step into the flying nuisances. He saw a flash of something from the corner of his eye. Something different that stood out from the moving scratches of light. He'd only glimpsed it for a fraction of a second. Just long enough to recognize the image.

It was the same horror-show version of his uncle he'd seen looming like a specter in the darkness of the Hollywood Squares backstage. The messy hair, the sneer, the narrowed eyes, and malevolent countenance were all accounted for in the fast blur of a face he saw. It was like Dorothy catching a glimpse of the wicked witch in the midst of the twister.

"Hey," Blake called out to the image. "Hey, what gives?"

"Blake, I'm behind you."

He whirled around to see this version of his uncle standing before him in the darkness. His hair was neat and combed. The ever-present smile firmly in place, and the maliciousness radiating from who or what he'd seen moments ago, was gone.

"What happened back there?" Blake fired off.

"I was about to ask you the same thing," the familiar man said, crossing his arms.

"Why? I was right there. I was about to get to him, and then . . . then . . ."

"Then what?"

"Then . . . he just disappeared. Dropped right out of sight and vanished into thin air."

"What? Are—are you sure?"

His younger-looking uncle furrowed his brow. The flesh folding to create lines that, years later, would become pronounced and permanent. It reminded Blake of his uncle before he supposedly died.

"Am I sure?" Blake was losing patience. "Yeah, I'm sure. And what the hell is going on with these shows anyway? People are dying, celebrities are mutating, and the audiences are full of deplorable, filthy, quasi-human, applause creatures. This isn't how things were happening when these shows, the *actual* shows were on. This is something . . . something else. Something bad and scary."

"Shit, I was afraid of that." The younger Uncle Gene sighed.

"Afraid of what?"

Blake suddenly heard a faint tune playing and looked over to see flashing lights in the distance fast approaching.

"We don't have mu—"

"Yeah, yeah," Blake interrupted. "No time, I know. But you have to tell me something useful here. I need help."

"I can only tell you what I know, and unfortunately from what you've told me, it seems you have some competition."

"Competition?"

"Something else is on the tape with us. Something that doesn't want your uncle to leave because that something is what trapped him here. I thought you would have gotten him out and both be safe before things *really* started getting bad, but I guess not. If you don't act fast, it's going to keep pulling the Uncle Gene you're here to save through the shows as quickly as possible to get to the end, thereby trapping you both."

"Something? You said *something* is on the tape? What the hell, man! Is that what stopped everything while I was backstage?"

"Yes, well . . . sort of. Things didn't stop, they paused."

"Pause? If it can do that, why not just fast-forward to the end and be done with it?"

The tune was louder, and the lights were brighter. Whatever was coming at them, it was coming fast.

"There are still some rules even *it* has to follow,"

the younger Uncle Gene said, looking nervously toward the approaching light. "The videotape must play all the way through. They can try to hide your uncle from you within the programs as they come. The only way they can move on sooner is by completely destroying the show as it's happening. There's no fast-forward, but the quicker it's able to pull things apart, the sooner it gets your uncle to the end. That means him, you, me, all of us are stuck here. Forever."

"What?"

"Blake, we don't have time fo—"

"You." Blake pointed, narrowly missing cutting the tip of his finger off on a passing patch of tracking. "What are *you* then? What do you get out of this? You'll still be on the tape afterwards no matter the outcome. So, where the hell are you existing in all of this?"

"I know, and those are fair questions. I'm an echo of your uncle's essence, so to speak. I was taped over, like I said, which gives me extremely limited and short access to you. I'm not your uncle in the true sense, but I am made up of his . . . energy. Which means I have a stake in wanting to get the present version of myself out of here.

Wouldn't you feel the same if *you* were in this situation?"

The two locked eyes, but their connection was short-lived. The lights were barreling down on them now. The music was loud enough for Blake to recognize it as the theme to *The Price Is Right*.

"Okay, okay," Blake said, shaking his head. "That almost makes sense in the loosest fashion imaginable, and mostly because I want it to, but that can't be all. There must be more to all this. You're just not telling me for whatever reason, so spill it."

"Sorry Blake."

The words were barely audible over the music now and the young version of Uncle Gene had already faded away as the darkness dissolved into the set of *The Price Is Right*.

13

THE ABRUPT CHANGE FROM dark nothingness to the full-blown illumination and loud intense sound was less jarring this time but still uncomfortable. Blake found himself in the audience, seated at the end of an aisle. He immediately realized things weren't right. The show itself was already in progress, but tuning in late was the least of his worries.

Blake scanned the audience looking for his uncle, but found himself surrounded by human-sized rat people. Each displayed the characteristics differently, with some having a mostly human face save for the extended nose and whiskers while others had pointed ears sprouting from their heads.

They all had pink segmented tails drooping from their asses dotted with random sprigs of wiry black hair.

The aroma of piss and fermenting trash assaulted Blake's senses, souring his stomach. His eyes watered, and he wiped them with the back of his hand then switched to breathing through his mouth. This only made things worse. The putrid stench traipsed heavily across his tongue coating the taste buds in a slippery layer of disgust that collided with the rising gorge of bile in his throat.

Blake stepped out into the aisle attempting to swallow back the impromptu surge of vomit and nearly slipped on a balled-up dirty diaper. The audience of rat-people clapped and hooted as he bent with his hands on his knees, explosively vomiting in the aisle.

"Blake Bitchman, come on down. You're the next contestant on *The Price Is Right*!"

Blake heard the announcer, but was too focused on stemming the tide of his sick to really listen. He found it odd when the name was repeated a few moments later.

"Blake? Blake Bitchman? BITCH-MAN? Hey Blake, come on down, you bitch!"

Out of vomit, Blake spit, trying to rid his mouth of the taste then noticed the rat faces turning in his direction. It was a few at first, then the rest all together at once.

"Yeah, they're looking at you, Blake. Blake Bitchman of Fuck-No Kansas. Get your bitch-ass on down, you bitch!"

The rat-people in the row closest to where he'd stumbled into the aisle screeched and squealed with glee, as if realizing they were in the presence of a huge celebrity. Before he could react, they lunged out and shoved him sending Blake skidding his way down the steps to the stage on his back. He tried to cry out, but the second stair knocked the wind out of him, and he sailed silently wailing the rest of the way.

He was spat from the audience and slid an additional ten feet across the stage floor on account of his momentum with help from the greasy puddle of sludge his ass splashed down in. The audience of humanoid vermin screeched with shrill glee, as Blake remained on his back for a moment before attempting to stand.

Above him, he saw tracking lines skirting between stage lights, reminding him of his task at hand. Whatever was trying to rip apart the tape, destroy the shows, and trap him and his Uncle Gene was doing a damn good job. Blake couldn't imagine this version of the show lasting long in the state things were presently. He sat up and felt around for a dry spot on the floor he could use to push himself up.

"Ha, ha, ha! There he goes ladies and gentlemen," the announcer's voice boomed down from speakers above. "I knew we'd get that little bitch down here sooner or later, Bob."

Bob. The announcer was referring to longtime show host and animal lover, Bob Barker, but when Blake turned to face him found it was a decidedly different version of the familiar man.

"Of course," Blake said to himself, taking in the scene before him.

The Bob Barker standing on stage was a dog-person in the same way the audience members were a human/rat hybrid. He was wearing a sharp blue suit and clutching his trademark long skinny microphone, only instead of a hand it was a paw wrapped around the base. The creature was human-like in the way it stood on two legs connected to a man-sized torso, but unlike the rat people, his face had only canine characteristics.

Blake wasn't great at pegging down dog breeds typically, but the host resembled the greyhound an ex-girlfriend of his owned. His snout was long and thin and the hair covering his face and paws was short and white. He was also smiling, and not in the way where it looks like a dog *happens* to be smiling either. This was an honest to goodness smile, and the only thing human-looking about his face. Although initially charming, the eerie, uncanny valley feel of what he was seeing made his head swim, and he turned away to keep from getting sick again.

"Hey there Blake," the dog-man of a host said. "Get your ass on over to contestant row with the rest of the bitches."

On his feet now, Blake looked to the podiums on his right and saw all but one occupied, which he assumed was where the host wanted him to go. Behind the remaining four were other dog-people, only unlike Barker they were dressed and styled to appear as women. Female dogs. Bitches.

"Time's a wasting, Blake," Barker said. "We've got a lot of game to get through."

Blake knew it wasn't true though, not with whatever was after his uncle doing its best to tear through the videotape until it reached the end. It already perverted the entirety of how the show was recorded originally, how this was occurring Blake was still unclear, but regardless, things were happening at an increasingly rapid pace. There wasn't time for him to play 'guess the price' to win his way into one of the main games, but he'd pretend while scrambling to think of a plan.

He shuffled his way to the empty podium between a Pekingese wearing a stunning red sundress and Dachshund dressed in a casual Betsy Johnson skirt and blouse. As he approached, their lipsticked mouths curved to form smiles he'd see in nightmares for the rest of his life. If he lived long enough to ever sleep again.

"Jesus Christ, Blake," Barker barked. "You go any slower, you'll be moving in reverse. Am I right, ladies and gentlemen?"

The rat men and women squealed with cartoonish laughter and applauded the host's remark, although Blake didn't remember the real Bob Barker ever roasting the contestants. He'd always wondered how well he would do if he were a *real* contestant on the show. It seemed easy as a spectator, but he never discounted the pressure of being put on the spot in the moment or the effect it can have when trying to think fast. This wasn't the time to test his price-guessing acuity though, he didn't plan on making it all the way to his designated podium.

Bob Barker turned his head to lick his shoulder for only a second, but it was all the time Blake needed to make a move. He turned on his heel and charged the stage, heading straight for Barker who had no time to react as Blake dipped down and buried his shoulder into the animal's chest. The force of impact sent the host flying backward with a yelp as Blake rushed by toward the curtain behind him. He grabbed the heavy fabric and pulled it from the hooks it hung from, revealing a ghastly sight it was concealing.

The first thing he saw was the puddle of blood, then the floating chunks of fur-covered flesh pulled his eyes to the source. A rat-person was on the ground having their neck savagely torn open by a cat wearing a designer gown. The feline creature lapped steadily at the waning flow of blood from the mortal wound and paused to look up at Blake.

She stood hissing a crimson spray in his direction, and he realized she was one of the spokesmodels for the show. More hissing joined in, and he looked to see two additional well-dressed cat-people coming at him from both sides brandishing red claws painted with dripping blood.

"Blake, no! What are you doing he—"

Just beyond the grisly scene was his Uncle Gene, only he'd been fastened to the bottom of a massive pegboard that made up his and his uncle's favorite game from the show, *Plinko*. One of the cat-ladies coming for Blake changed course, leaping instead toward his bound uncle slashing at his face before he could finish.

To play *Plinko*, a contestant would start by guessing prices of small market items and receive *Plinko* discs for each correct answer. The discs were roughly the size of a hockey puck but only a quarter-inch thick. The lucky contestant would then climb the fifteen-foot-high pegboard, stand behind it, and drop the discs down one at a time where they would bounce off the pegs as they fell, changing direction sometimes drastically depending on the angle of approach.

At the bottom were sections labeled with a dollar

amount the contestant would win if their disc ended its journey there. There were also spaces that would negate their total earnings or bring the player all the way back to zero.

There was not another game in all the game shows Blake watched with his uncle that he wanted to play more than *Plinko*. It was something he'd fantasized about as a kid and dreamt of making his own *Plinko* board so he could practice at home. He planned to learn exactly where to drop the discs, so he always won the highest amount of money. Then, when he was old enough, he'd go on and compete as the top *Plinko* player in the world.

Standing before the game that brought him so much joy and hope as a child should've had a dramatically different effect on Blake, but what he saw was a version of the game he'd never want to play. Rather than the pegs being spaced evenly across the board making the disc's journey random and unpredictable, they were positioned to funnel it directly down into the space occupied by his uncle's head. No matter where it was dropped from, it would always find its way to the same spot.

Blake noticed the 'o' in *Plinko* painted at the top of the board was drawn with pointy barbs poking out from the letter, and he knew exactly what it was depicting. They weren't going to drop flimsy wooden discs on Uncle Gene's head. They were dropping saw blades instead. Another feline spokesmodel appeared at the top of the board, poised to drop one of the circular blades.

"Uncle Gene! Hold on, I'm coming."

A barrage of barking came from backstage where he'd shoved Bob Barker, and a moment later the curtain parted as five large dog-men wearing shirts with the word 'security' printed in capital letters ran through. Blake knew right away they were Doberman Pinschers since a neighbor of his had one back when he was in elementary school.

That dog terrified Blake and chased him home from the bus stop after school nearly every day for an entire semester. The neighbor would laugh and say the dog would not hurt him, but Blake knew better. He'd seen the look in the dog's eye, watched saliva drip from its pointy teeth as it waited for him to get off the bus. He knew in his heart the dog would tear him apart if he ever got a hold of him, which luckily never happened.

Watching these hybrid dog beasts charging his way, now knowing their intention was to tear him apart, brought on a crippling flash of déjà vu. The musculature of their chests and arms rippled through their shirts as they ran.

The cat-woman who'd been dining on the rat-man's neck stepped toward Blake while one of her associates came from the right. The cat-lady who'd attacked his uncle stayed back guarding his prone form shackled to the perverted *Plinko* board. The Doberman security team was approaching fast from his left, barking loud enough to pierce the frenzied cheering of the audience. Blake lunged forward at the incoming cat-woman and caught his first break.

The creature slipped in the blood, fell backward over the corpse, and screeched when its head bounced hard against the tile of the studio floor. Distracted, the other cat-woman tripped over her own tail when she turned, and Blake sailed by, narrowly missing them both. He landed just shy of the blood puddle, surprising himself with his own dexterity and luck until his other foot came down, skidded out in front of him, and he fell backward.

The cat-woman guarding his uncle leapt to attack as well, and he watched her fly over him, looking down in angry confusion before colliding with the security team sending them back into the tangled pile of cats, dogs, and rat parts. Blake landed on his back, but not too hard, and slid forward, coming to a stop at his uncle's feet.

"Jesus Christ, Blake," Uncle Gene said, looking down at him, blood running from the slashes across his lips. "You really fucked up."

"Nice to see you too," Blake said, taking longer than he wanted to get to his feet.

"Go! Get away from me."

Ignoring his uncle's protests, Blake examined the man's bonds. He expected to find something holding him in place, like rope, or leather straps, or maybe chains, but there was nothing he could see. It appeared his uncle was stuck to the vertical wooden game board with adhesive, as if he'd backed up against a wall of flypaper.

On closer inspection, he found his Uncle Gene was indeed glued to the *Plinko* board from the back of his head down to his heels. Even his hands were attached palm down. Veins bulge through the skin of his fingers as he strained to rip them from the ultra-sticky surface.

Blake grabbed him by the shoulders and pulled, but the glue held fast, and his uncle cried out in pain. He didn't know how he'd be able to remove him without leaving a layer of skin behind. It didn't help that his uncle was actively resisting, pushing back harder against the adhesive-covered wall. Blake glanced over his shoulder and saw the security dogs detangling themselves from the chaos of the cat collision while the spokesmodels hissed and yowled, digging in with their claws.

"Look, Uncle Gene we do—"

"Leave me here," his uncle shouted in his face. "Go now! Before it's too late."

From above, Blake heard a distinct 'plinking' sound, the noise from which the etymology of the game's name was derived. It was the sound of wooden discs hitting metal pegs on their way down hence, *Plinko*. This time, though, the 'plink' was a bit higher pitched, because instead of a flat wooden disc making its way down the board in the direction of his uncle's head, it was a round metal saw blade. Stage lights reflected off its shiny surface save for the outer circle of diamond-sharpened blades which were stained dark red.

"Fuck!" Blake shouted, trying to pull his uncle from the board again. "If you know a trick to get unstuck, now would be the time to tell me. I know you think you don't want to go with me. I know you think you belong here, but you won't be going anywhere if we don't get you down from here."

Plink. Plink. Plink.

The saw blade was almost halfway down when a second one was dropped.

"Belong here?" Uncle Gene said. "I *know* I don't belong here, and neither do you. That's why I'm telling you to get the he— Oh shit, watch out!"

The warning came a moment too late, as Blake felt the sudden explosion of pain in his shoulder. He'd never been bitten by a dog before, nor had he experienced the intensity of having his flesh pierced by multiple sharp objects at once. It was a confusing sensation, to say the least. He felt pressure and heat in his shoulder, then abrasive throbbing, shot from the area down the small of his back and up his spine.

Shock crippled his vocal cords as he fell forward into his captive uncle's chest, mouthing a silent scream. Frenzied commotion erupted behind him, and the fanged jaws detached from Blake's shoulder followed by a whimper that was quickly drowned out by the growing swell of feral hissing. He used his uncle's body to regain his balance and braced for another excruciating bite while struggling to keep his footing.

When it didn't come, Blake pushed himself off his uncle and whirled around, ready to fend off the next attack until he saw the utter calamity behind him. The Doberman security guard responsible for chomping Blake's shoulder was face down on the floor being pulled back into the escalating violence by one of the cats. The guard struggled unsuccessfully to gain purchase on the slick tile of the stage while trying to escape his feline attacker's grasp but a moment later was back in the fray.

A puddle of blood spanned from one side of the stage to the other, and chunks of fur and flesh from the writhing mass of cat-on-dog assault seemed to have become an entity unto itself. What was happening out in the audience was even worse.

Tracking lines shot back and forth through the aisles, randomly slashing open bodies of dirty rat-people, spilling their foul innards into the already shockingly powerful filth of the studio audience area. Severed limbs flew across rows, while several instantaneous decapitations sent sprays of blood into the air like a synchronized water feature display from the fountain of a fancy hotel.

Even so, Blake still heard the *plink, plink, plink* clicking off the few moments he had left to free his uncle. A ferocious and rabid Bob Barker shot out from behind a curtain, running on all fours, snarling as he leapt to join the fight. He caught one of the cat-people by the throat in his jaws and took them to the ground, shaking it violently by the neck. A moment later, the host was swallowed by a swarm of cats and howled in agony as their claws ripped through his suit into his flesh.

Plink. Plink. Plink.

"Uncle Gene," Blake yelled, turning back to his uncle.

The first saw blade was a mere three plinks away from burying itself in his uncle's skull, but the one behind it was acting differently. Halfway down, it stood up on its side cutting *into* the *Plinko* board itself. The blade bit easily into the wood, pulling it apart like tissue to reveal the cosmic darkness of the videotape void behind.

Plink. Plink.

"Shit! No! No! No!"

Blake leapt at the board, with arm out, attempting to reach the blade and stop it with his bare hand. Even if it was cut to shit or severed completely, it was better than having it lodged in his uncle's brain. Blake stumbled in his attempt and the final *plink* sounded as his hand contacted the blade a moment too late. He thought for sure the hesitation cost him his uncle's life until realizing the blade had stopped on its own. It was only an inch from striking and appeared to be hovering in place. Something else was happening.

"Blake go!"

Uncle Gene shouted; his eyes crossed, trying to look up unsuccessfully at the blade, wondering himself why it hadn't hit him already. Blake *could* see, though, and realized what was happening. The blade wasn't stuck and only appeared to hover in place because it was being sucked into the portal above. There, it remained suspended for another half second before shooting up and through the tear in the cosmically cataclysmic reality.

Whatever was hunting Blake and his uncle had succeeded in destroying this section of the tape and was attempting to pull Uncle Gene through to the next show. The lights across the studio flashed with a nauseating strobe effect, and the brutal animalistic carnage now appeared in gruesome still images. Blake saw it wasn't a malfunction of the lights making them flash, but large patches of tracking. Flying scratches of light were cutting away large chunks of ceiling, opening more holes into the darkness.

Something like a wolf's howl cut through the rowdy sounds of animalistic combat and cries of pain, an incoming addition to the scuffle Blake wanted no part of. He reached for his uncle hoping to keep him from being pulled in after the saw blade, an effort he thought would be aided by the strength of the adhesive holding him to the board. He was wrong, and Uncle Gene's legs suddenly became unstuck and flew out kicking Blake in the groin. He stumbled back and fell to his knees with a whimper, as all he could do was watch his uncle's body slide up the pegboard toward the portal. As the top of his head reached the opening, he made a final effort to communicate with Blake.

"Don't follow me!" His voice broke as he tried to project enough to be heard over the surrounding chaos. "And whatever you do, don't listen to th—"

Uncle Gene was pulled through the portal before he could finish, and the *Plinko* board collapsed in on itself as the entire structure was sucked through, including Blake.

14

BLAKE WAS BACK IN THE staticky darkness watching flashes of razor-sharp tracking lines chase each other away. He wasn't alone either. The other version of Uncle Gene stood in front of him scowling, arms crossed.

"You're fucking this up," younger Uncle Gene said. "You know that, right? There's not much tape left and—"

"Yeah, yeah," Blake interrupted, cupping his groin, amazed at how quickly the pain had vanished. "I know this already. If we have such precious little time, why don't you start telling me something new?"

Young Uncle Gene narrowed his eyes and sucked his teeth with a sharp click. He started to resemble the sinister-looking person Blake glimpsed peeking from the darkness of the Hollywood Squares backstage. Young Uncle Gene's voice was sharp and pointed. His tone dripped with venom. Blake never heard his uncle curse in such a way. At worst, he'd heard him use 'shit' a handful of times and only as an exclamation of excitement, never out of anger.

"You still don't get it, do you?" Young Uncle Gene said. "Despite what you've already experienced, you don't grasp the seriousness of your situation, the gravity?"

Blake shook his head and shrugged while tracking lines flashed across the space between them as if trying to corral the men like a referee keeping boxing opponents separated.

"Just take a closer look this time," he continued. "The window will be there. You just have to find it, and when you do, it'll show you."

"Show me what?"

Young Uncle Gene said nothing, and Blake pressed further.

"Back in that last game, Uncle Gene, the *real* Uncle Gene, was trying to get me to leave him. He wanted *me* to get away."

"I told you that would happen."

"Yeah, but you said he thought he was supposed to be here, like he'd been tricked into believing it or something. But he told me he *knew* he wasn't supposed to be here. Made it sound like he wanted to leave, but couldn't for some reason."

"And?"

"*And* he was trying to tell me something else before he was pulled through," Blake continued. "He said there was someone I shouldn't trust but was gone before he could say who. Do you know who he was talking about? Was he telling me not to trust . . . you?"

"Find the window, Blake," young Uncle Gene said with a smile. "Look through, and you'll see exactly what he meant."

A gaggle of tracking lines threw static across the space between the two men, and young Uncle Gene flickered, then vanished in their wake. Blake suddenly found himself standing in front of a stack of colorful boxes. As he oriented himself to the abrupt change, he realized he knew *exactly* where he was. The cereal aisle of a supermarket.

15

BLAKE FOLLOWED THE SOUND of applause down the aisle. He had an inkling as to where he was, and as he emerged into a brightly lit open area, his suspicion was confirmed. He was on the lone, successful, grocery store game show *Supermarket Sweep*.

While the show had been on for a number of years, it was hardly a classic. Though initially launched in the late sixties, it was *barely* on before they pulled it not to be brought back until the nineties, where it finally found success. It didn't rank among Uncle Gene's favorites, but he'd made the effort to attend as a studio audience member twice. His uncle was more of a passive watcher of the show, while Blake would be glued to the screen for its entirety. When it was on, Uncle Gene would tidy up and do other small chores, not parking himself on the couch until the final showdown at the end of each episode.

The show pit three pairs of contestants against each other, competing for the chance to out-shop one another in the grocery store set constructed on a soundstage for a chance to win cash, prizes, and even the groceries. Teams were comprised of married couples, siblings, parents with their adult child, and in rare cases, best friends.

"Ha ha. Hey there Blake, don't wander off just yet. You'll have plenty of time to shop later."

The host of the show, David Ruprecht, stood before a podium at the center stage. He wore a brightly colored sweater covered in random patterns that screamed 1990's. Across from him were three contestant podiums manned by the competing teams. Behind the one furthest to the left stood a portly man and woman wearing nametags that said 'Bill' and 'Doris', respectively. It looked like they were frowning, but it was simply how their faces appeared when at rest. Their clothes were mismatched and ill-fitting, and despite the game having yet to start, they were both sweating like it was an interrogation.

The team at the center podium was comprised of two women with red curly hair and identical faces covered in an unfortunate smattering of freckles. Twins, he guessed, and they too wore stern expressions, though Blake realized they were glaring at him for slowing the progress of the game.

A single person stood behind the third podium wearing a nametag written in thick black print that said, 'Uncle Gene'. Blake looked down at his chest to see he was also wearing a similar tag scrawled with his own name. Things were looking up. He'd found his uncle right away with only ten feet of space between them. This time the distance wasn't covered in rotting food, animal waste, or bloody carnage.

Blake stepped quickly over to his uncle, scanning the audience on the way, squinting to see past the stage lights. As far as he could tell there were people in the seats, actual, real, *human* people. No mutated animal hybrids. No distorted nightmare creatures. No ALFs or heads in jars. The audience was seemingly comprised of normal people varying in size and shape, but as people do and not monsters.

Blake looked at the smiling host whose expression wasn't smeared absurdly across his face. It was a normal smile. Pleasant. Inviting. Another quick take of the other contestants revealed further normality in that, while they may not be happy or esthetically pleasing, they weren't dead-eyed ghouls shoving handfuls of melted sugar in their faces. They were people. They were all just people.

For the first time since he'd been pulled into this backward nightmare of a situation, Blake felt the smallest amount of hope. This time, there was seemingly nothing posing as an obstacle to keep him from saving his uncle. Even if the man refused to go, Blake was prepared to throw him over his shoulder and run like Hell, which is where it felt like they were.

He stepped behind the podium next to his uncle, and the excitement froze in his stomach, prickling his bowels with icy sharp tendrils. Despite there being nothing keeping him from escaping with his uncle in tow, he had no idea *where* he was supposed to take him. He'd been operating under the assumption the younger version of his uncle would've either told him by now or would pop out from a hidden manhole when the time came to point the way.

Blake looked around and saw the word '*EXIT*' glowing in the darkness on the far side of the stage behind the host. It might be on the nose, but he figured it was as good a place as any to start. He'd grab his uncle, drag him toward the sign, and if it led to nowhere, he'd figure it out then. Nothing about this had been easy or normal so far and this appeared to be both. It couldn't last long, though, and he needed to act before the other shoe dropped.

"Hey Uncle Gene," Blake said, stepping beside him behind the podium. "Holy shit, am I glad to see you. Look, I know you told me to—"

"I'm sorry, son," Uncle Gene said, turning to Blake putting his finger against his lips. "I think you have me confused with someone else. Now, quiet down so we can start the game."

Blake was taken aback.

"What? No, Uncle Gene, it's me, Blake. Look."

He tugged at his nametag, then went to grab his uncle's to show him what it said, but he slapped his hand away.

"I don't know who you are, or who you think I am, but you're wrong. Now quiet down so we can play."

The host was explaining rules to one of the games, but it registered only as background noise to Blake. He was expecting his uncle to resist, even argue, and try to fight back. He didn't think the man would not only not recognize him but also deny his own identity despite wearing a nametag that said otherwise. If he didn't know who Blake was, why were they competing as a team on *Supermarket Sweep*? His uncle didn't even like the show. Blake could sense the shroud of normalcy beginning to slip from their surroundings, taking his lone ember of hope with it.

"Would you two shut up over there?"

The ginger-headed twins at the podium next to him fixed their identical snarls firmly upon him and his uncle. Blake didn't know which one had scalded him, but it didn't matter. This would not be the smash-and-grab type of scenario he thought he'd lucked into. He'd play the game for the time being, and hope he figured something out before whatever was after them, pulled his uncle through another rip in the videotape.

"Alright everyone, let's settle down," Ruprecht said, his smile maintaining its original size and placement. "Save it for the aisles."

"You're dead meat, dickweed."

The twin closest to Blake whispered the threat and ran a finger quickly across her neck in a cutting motion. He turned back to his uncle, who was staring at the host in rapt attention, hanging on his every word while aggressively tuning out Blake's presence.

He quickly surmised the best time to make his move was during one of the games that involved physically going out into the aisles to shop. It would give him the ability to run around without being stopped or tackled immediately. If he managed to put his uncle into one of the grocery carts, he could easily rush him across the stage to the 'EXIT' door and hope for the best.

It wasn't much of a plan, but it was better than nothing, especially when the whole show could go to shit at any moment. Things were mostly fine now, but soon the floor would turn to lava, or a swarm of beetles would eat their way out of David Ruprecht's face while blades of light flew through the studio, ripping audience members apart.

To gain access to one of the carts, he and his uncle would have to answer a question correctly to qualify for the challenge. Blake struggled to wrangle his attention back toward what the host was saying when Uncle Gene slammed his hand down on the buzzer of their podium.

"Mama's little baby loves shortening, shortening," his uncle shouted.

"That is correct!" The host said. "Great job Uncle Gene. Now, which one of you will shop for the bonus?"

It took a second to realize his uncle had answered a question, thereby unknowingly advancing Blake's plan. He quickly spoke up, cutting the man off to claim the honor himself.

"Me!" Blake practically screamed. "I will. I'll do it. I got it."

He made his way around the podium before Uncle Gene could protest and headed over to meet the host at center stage amidst a light smattering of applause from the audience.

"Okay Blake, that's the kind of enthusiasm we like to see," Ruprecht said. "Now, for this challenge you'll have sixty seconds to find four different products by following clues attached to ea—"

"Yep, sounds good. I got it."

Blake elbowed past the host and rushed toward a cart waiting for him where he'd entered at the opening of the cereal aisle. He grabbed the handle, whirled it around toward his uncle, but was stopped short by a cameraman.

It was one of several positioned around the set to follow contestants through the store as they shopped, capturing all the action of the game. Blake hadn't counted on having to deal with these obstacles, but was confident he could navigate them successfully and get to his uncle. He jerked back and moved to the left with his body while pushing the cart to the right, trying to trip him up.

The cameraman stumbled and caught his balance quickly, but the small misstep provided the opening he needed. Blake happened to look into the camera as he lunged forward and stopped short at what he saw. He let go of the cart and walked slowly toward the cameraman, staring directly into the lens.

"Window," Blake said. "Look through the window."

16

BLAKE WAS LOOKING INTO his apartment from the perspective of the television screen and now understood what the other version of his uncle meant by 'window'. He recognized what he was seeing as his own living room, *his* couch, *his* lamp, *his* coffee table. What he didn't recognize were the two men sitting on *his* couch with their feet up on *his* coffee table, staring into *his* television screen at him. A black zipped up garment bag lay draped over one of the armrests Blake didn't recognize as belonging to him.

The men were similar in build, both with short brown hair and mustaches wearing matching gray coveralls that concealed any other distinguishing features. They looked dazed, or stoned, or both, and Blake briefly wondered if this was how he looked when watching television. A flicker of realization registered on one of the men's faces as he appeared to lock eyes with Blake.

He taped the man next to him and pointed at the screen. The other man, annoyed at first, realized what his counterpart was communicating and smiled. He also pointed while obviously laughing, though Blake heard no sound.

"Hello?" He said into the camera, moving his face even closer. "Can you hear me? I can't hear you."

The men in his living room leapt to their feet, howling with laughter. He watched their lips articulate quips between guffaws, extending the round of belly laughs by trying to one-up each others apparent hilariously insulting zingers.

The first man reached behind, pulled something from his back pocket, and shook it at the screen. It was the remote-control Blake found at his uncle's place, the one with the melted 'power' button. The man then extended the hand not holding the remote and gave Blake the finger.

"Hey!" Blake shouted at the lens. "Hey! Fuck you! Get out of my apartment!"

Panic and instinct took over, as Blake cocked his arm back, intending to punch his way through the lens to get to them, but the cameraman easily dodged his clunky telegraphed attempt. The misplaced momentum of his follow through carried him to the ground where his face smacked the tile floor. He saw stars but fought off the blackness, threatening to close off his vision. He willed away the swirling darkness and forced himself to his feet, desperately searching for the 'window'.

The camera man backed six feet to his right, keeping the lens leveled on Blake. Even at the distance, he could still see his living room through the convex glass. The men were doubled over in laughter after seeing him eat shit, as his face throbbed from kissing the stage tile. Now Blake's rage began to bubble over. He shook off a bout of dizziness, went for the camera again, but stopped when his uncle called out.

"What are you doing, you idiot? You're ruining the game."

"But . . . Uncle Gene," Blake huffed, catching his breath. "My apartment . . . I can see . . . they . . . they're in there."

"Have you lost your—"

Uncle Gene froze mid-sentence and the muscles in his face tensed like he was having a stroke or experiencing a mild electric shock, but the spell seemed to pass as soon as it came on. He swung his head back and forth, as his eyes darted around, taking in the surroundings like it was all new to him, like he was seeing it for the first time. When Uncle Gene saw Blake, a brief look of recognition was immediately swallowed by concern.

"Apartment?" Uncle Gene said. "Did you say they're in your apartment? *Already?*"

"I . . . they . . . yes. What?"

Blake tried his best but found it hard to put a sentence together with the painful buzzing in his head. It was getting harder to fight off the effects of the injury, and he suddenly badly wanted to go to sleep. He gestured to the camera again, its operator planted firmly in place holding his ground, poised to take evasive action if needed.

"Damnit Blake, I tried to tell you not to follow me," Uncle Gene said, leaving the podium.

"Hey, you ass-hats," one of the redheaded twins yelled. "We said stop fucking this up for us!"

"Yeah, we came here to shop and win." This protest lobbed from the triple-chinned donut-hole of a woman wearing the 'Doris' nametag at the far podium. "Go kick their asses so we can play, Bill.

Doris squawked at her husband pointing to Blake and Uncle Gene. The man responded with a shrug before lumbering around the podium to heed her command. The husband, Bill, cracked his knuckles and massaged his fists as he followed along behind the twins.

"Okay everyone, let's just settle down," the host finally piped up. "We love good old-fashioned spirited competition, but this is, well; this is a bit much."

"Can it, Ruprecht!" One of the twins yelled.

She snatched a can of cream corn from an end cap and chucked it at the host with the velocity and accuracy of a major league pitcher. It struck his face just below his right eye, cracking it open, then spun off toward the audience spraying a creamy yellow mist behind. David Ruprecht stumbled but appeared to catch his balance, swaying slowly from side to side, staring off into space.

The can left a deep indentation which quickly went from pink to red to purple just before his eye began to sag. It moved slowly at first, creeping from its home with caution, but the bone structure designed to hold it in place was destroyed. The ocular orb dropped from its damaged socket with an unceremonious plop and dangled lightly, kissing against the sunken side of his face.

Ruprecht's mouth fell open, but he could only mumble wet choking sounds as the trickle of blood from his ear became a steady flow. The badly injured host, slowly tipping forward, when a second can, green beans this time, collided with the center of his face hard enough to reverse his trajectory. Now he was falling backward with blood rocketing in long crimson arcs from both sides of his nose, which had been turned inside out forcefully relocating his frontal lobe.

Blake didn't see the host hit the floor, having turned just in time to duck an incoming can meant for him, but he heard the hollow *thunk* of his head meeting the floor and the crunch of his skull yielding to the impact. Before he could retaliate, his uncle shoved him into the closest aisle.

"Get down," Uncle Gene growled.

Blake had little choice in the matter as he stumbled, tripping over himself and falling again. He managed to land on his shoulder this time, which exploded in pain and dislocated on impact, but at least his head was saved from additional trauma. He slid three or four feet down the slick polished tile and the view of his pursuers was temporarily blocked. Blake went to push himself up but collapsed back to the floor, his shoulder burning angrily and hot with pain.

The sound of shattering glass came from beyond the aisle, followed by what sounded to Blake like sheet metal being torn. The angry cries of confrontation became screams of fear and confusion before the roar of rushing air drowned everything out. It was already happening, and he was too late. He knew it felt too easy.

Blake clung to a lower shelf lined in bags of dry rice with his right hand, using it to pull himself up while the left one dangled useless and limp. He got to his feet just as the other contestants, minus Uncle Gene, rounded the corner and charged toward him down the aisle. All he could do was hold tight to the shelf with his bad shoulder turned away from them and brace for the attack, but they ran by without so much as looking at him.

The only thing Blake felt was the rush of air as they blew past, but then realized it was the vacuum suction of the portal he assumed had opened just beyond the aisle. An ear splitting sharp crack, like the frozen surface of an icy pond breaking, came from the direction the contestants were fleeing.

"Uncle Gene," he called, struggling to project over the increasing volume of rushing air. "Uncle Gene, I'm coming! Just hang on. Please!"

Blake mustered his remaining strength and charged down the aisle toward the stage hoping his uncle hadn't been pulled through to the next show yet. He rounded the corner and saw he was indeed still there, or at least most of him. It was hard to tell exactly what he was seeing at first as a herd of tracking lines danced erratically, blocking his view, but they seemed to part especially for him as if presenting a grand reveal.

The cameraman was now a hybrid, creature-like representation of his vocation, having become half man and half camera, only not exactly. He hadn't transformed harmoniously into a nightmarish amalgamation of man and machine, but instead the camera looked to have been forcefully crammed in the space between the man's shoulders previously occupied by his head.

The camera was lodged three-quarters into the crowded body cavity with the lens pointed straight up at the ceiling. Slick chunks of glistening moist gore ran down his shoulders and chest, mixing with a puddle of piss at his feet.

As horrid as the cameraman's predicament, it wasn't the most disturbing part of what was happening. The lower half of Uncle Gene from his waist down was sticking out from the camera lens like a mechanized anaconda was in the process of swallowing him. Roughly six feet above his uncle's feet was the swirling rush of darkness of the portal. A bizarre tug-of-war was going on with his uncle as the rope, and if he didn't act fast, he'd lose him again.

Blake rushed, overreaching for his uncle's legs, suddenly remembering only one of his arms worked. The other bounced limply, shooting mini-bursts of pain through his shoulder with each step. He grit his teeth against the sting and latched on to his uncle, wrapping the good arm around his waist. Blake pulled back with all his might using his body as dead weight to try and wrestle his uncle from both opposing grasps. Suddenly, it started to work.

He could feel his uncle's body slide out from the camera lens and, as it did, he also managed to wrench him away from the pull of the portal overhead. Blake didn't realize his uncle wasn't being pulled from the camera lens by him. He was being pushed out by something from inside. He continued to hold tight with one arm as the upper half of Uncle Gene spilled out, taking them both to the floor. The fall inadvertently pushed Blake's arm back into the socket, which was more painful than when it popped out of place. The two struggled to detangle and get to their feet while staying low enough to avoid being caught in the portal's suction.

"Stay down, Blake."

Uncle Gene pushed on his nephew's chest to keep him down, but he was looking up at something else. Blake struggled, then followed his uncle's sightline and froze. Sticking out of the camera lens, much like a genie escaping their lamp, was the upper half of *the* other version of Uncle Gene, the one who was supposed to be helping him.

"Uh, uh, uh," younger Uncle Gene said, wagging his finger. "You know you can't get out that way. Your nephew is new here, but I would've expected you to know better."

Uncle Gene lunged at the half of a man protruding from the camera, but a patch of tracking ran across the floor in front of him, slicing open another hole into darkness. Luckily, his uncle could jump back before falling in, but the reprieve was temporary as more scratchy razor lights tore into the floor. Uncle and nephew suddenly found themselves trapped on a small section of stage surrounded by gaping bottomless holes.

Blake was on his feet now standing shoulder to shoulder with his uncle trying to keep as much space as possible between them and the edge. Across the chasm of portals, something was happening to younger Uncle Gene. He was getting bigger, changing, becoming something else.

The camera burst apart, scattering shards of glass and plastic across the stage to be sucked into the closest hole in the floor. The heavily ravaged body of the cameraman was flattened under the sudden explosion of size and girth in a final act of disrespect. The pulverized mush of his insides exited his body like a cinder block dropped on a tube of toothpaste.

The still-growing creature no longer resembled Blake's Uncle as it swelled to an unrecognizable blob covered in rippled flesh that glistened like oil in water. Semi-amorphous limbs were muscular and chiseled one moment, then flabby and gelatinous the next. The younger uncle's face was a melty mess of misplaced features fighting each other to become permanent fixtures on the shifting visage. His legs fused together making his lower half like that of a snake or giant earthworm.

The newly formed tail smacked into the closest mock-grocery aisle, knocking it into the next one, obliterating them both. Paper towels and toilet paper rolls rained down like confetti, and a powdery plume of detergent erupted from the mess, making it difficult to breathe. Luckily, the cloud of soap was quickly sucked out into the VHS void by way of over a dozen portals, with more being ripped and torn into existence every few seconds.

The thing that had been younger Uncle Gene towered over them while its flesh remained in a state of perpetual motion. It writhed and undulated in waves like liquid smoke, incapable of settling on one single form. A garbled roar came from a hole that opened in the center of the creature's face and promptly sealed off by a cascading waterfall of melting pliable flesh. A second bigger maw yawned open through the muck to the left of its closed counterpart, belching the remainder of the roar cut short.

Two glowing red orbs pushed out from the shifting mix as well, casting a red pallor across parts of the stage that still existed. Blake looked toward the audience and saw the people were gone with each seat now occupied by honey baked hams. Some were bigger than others and some looked like they may just be a hog shank but all ham, nonetheless. Things were getting bad fast, and the two of them were seconds away from either falling into dark nothingness or being pulverized by the churning bulk of what younger Uncle Gene had become. Either way, at least Blake and his uncle were together this time, or they were until crackling lines of tracking ripped through the patch of tile between them.

The small bit of floor they'd been standing on became two smaller pieces that tipped back under their weight, and they began to fall away from each other. Blake reached out to grab the hand his uncle was emphatically thrusting his way but hadn't been quick enough. His fingertips grazed the back of his uncle's hand, as the two toppled off in different directions, separated once again. Blake cried out in frustration desperately grasping hands of empty air cursing his incessant failure.

The monstrous blob-thing howled as Blake toppled end over end into VHS oblivion, wondering if they'd reached the end of the tape, if he'd blown his last chance to save Uncle Gene and himself. The roar of the creature came from all directions as he continued to spin off into the nebulous ether.

The cacophonous cry of the beast reached an uncomfortable level, swirling in Blake's head as he reflected on a lifetime of doubt and uncertainty. His life had been a string of wishy-washy, non-committal, half-assed decisions with little to no follow up and zero accountability. He'd made his way, taking the path of least resistance, settling for what came rather than taking action to go out and get what he wanted, and his life reflected as much.

His apartment used to belong to a friend who was moving out, so Blake moved in and took over. The furniture, with the exception of his bed and television, had all been left behind. Blake assimilated himself to the place with barely a ripple of disruption. He took a temp position at a call center because the building was down the street from his apartment, and due to a mistake in the system somewhere along the line, the temporary position became permanent. They continued to schedule him, so he kept going. That was two and a half years ago, and nothing had changed.

A string of glinting sharp-edged tracking lines shot past his face, missing the tip of his nose by half an inch. Something clamped down on his right forearm and he jolted, thinking it'd been severed until he saw his uncle's hand holding tight. Blake didn't know if they'd been falling or floating or a bit of both, but he suddenly felt like everything was slowing down. A moment later he was standing in the patchy darkness across from his Uncle Gene.

17

THE GIANT BEAST WAS NOWHERE IN SIGHT, but the echo of its tremendous wail carried through the darkness yet to decay. Blake looked up expecting to see it falling mouth-first down onto them, but he and his uncle stood in the buzzing darkness alone.

"What the hell are you doing here?" Uncle Gene snapped.

"You know, you keep asking and I keep saying the same thing." Blake's tone smoldered with annoyance. "I'm supposed to be saving you, or at least that's what I've been told by whatever the hell that thing was before it went all nightmare fuel on us up there. Now, I honestly have no idea what I'm doing here."

"Goddamnit," Uncle Gene said. "They weren't supposed to drag anyone else into this. How . . . how'd you get here anyway?"

"*Who* wasn't supposed to drag anyone else into . . . *what?* Where is this?"

"Sorry. I'm sorry, Blake." Uncle Gene massaged his temples and softened his tone. "I'm not mad at you."

He stepped forward, threw his arms around his nephew, and squeezed. Blake was hesitant to reciprocate, half-afraid it wasn't his actual uncle but another lookalike. An evil avatar waiting to get a hold of him before taking its grotesque true form as it absorbed him into its carnivorous undulating flesh. It only took a moment to know for certain the man embracing him was indeed the real Uncle Gene, and Blake enthusiastically returned the hug. He didn't realize how badly he needed one until that very moment.

"This place," Uncle Gene started as he pulled back from the hug. "This place is cursed, or more accurately, it *is* a curse, but not for us."

"Curse?"

"This . . . all of this," Uncle Gene gestured at the darkness surrounding them. "Everything you've seen so far, every place you've been in here, it's all for him. It's Mirim's curse."

Blake's mind flashed through all the times his uncle had mentioned Mirim throughout the years. Now that he thought about it, he had no clue if they were a friend, lover, work associate, or other form of acquaintance. Uncle Gene had never given any details regarding what his relationship to Mirim was when Blake was growing up, no specifics into who this mystery person may be, which was most likely exactly how he wanted it.

"You mean your friend or whatever, Mirim? That Mirim is here?"

"They are *not* my friend," his uncle said with indignance. "That thing up there, that . . . monster. That's Mirim."

Blake didn't think he could be more confused by the situation until receiving that bit of information. Was his uncle in cahoots with a monster from another realm? Did he run in secret, mystic, occult circles? Was he a practitioner of the dark arts focused on summoning creatures from hell, or the void, or wherever? Did he truly have no idea who his uncle was?

"He looked like you to me," Blake said. "He said

he still had some of your essence or something, told me he was still part of you. What the hell is this, *really?* What's going on and where are we?"

"There's . . . well, sort of a lot to unpack regarding your concerns."

"I would say I'm more than just concerned. He, Mirim, said you were stuck on this videotape, and that I could save you if I got to you before the tape ended. He said he was supposed to be helping but didn't tell me any information I could truly use. I only just realized I didn't know how to get you out once I found you, and now that I have, I'm assuming you don't know either. So, if you don't mind, begin with the unpacking please."

"I'll do my best," Uncle Gene started. "But we don't have much time before the next show on the tape starts, the *last* show on the tape."

"I've been hearing that line since I got here." Blake was irritated and flustered now. "Stop wasting time telling me how little time we have, and just tell me what I need to know."

"I found Mirim on the tape years ago." Uncle Gene sighed; his shoulders sagged. "I'd bought a stack of used VHS tapes at an estate sale intending to record my game shows over whatever had been on them prior, which is exactly what I did until I reached *this* tape. The ones before it contained old sitcoms, some westerns, a few popular movies from when they'd played on network television, complete with commercials and all. I didn't pay much attention. I just rewound the tapes and recorded over them.

When I used this tape, *Mirim's* tape, everything changed. After I'd filled it with my game shows Mirim appeared before the tape ended. They spoke directly to me from the television, told me about the curse and how the two of us could help one another. I should've shut it off right then and burned that tape. Of course, I found out later, much like a Ouija board, the tape couldn't be burned, but I still should've gotten rid of it."

The beast's scream had faded into the rush of white noise, and an approaching wave of faraway applause could be heard over the staticky din. Blake sensed his uncle's rising anxiety as he spoke quickly, trying to finish the story.

"I didn't have to work anymore, Blake; I didn't have to do anything, really. All I had to do was allow myself to be put on the tape when I died, but not until then. Simple as that. Mirim would make it so

I could go see live game shows anytime I wanted and not have to worry about, well; anything. Hell, I can't remember the last time I paid a bill or gave my landlord rent money, and no one's ever asked for it. Mirim was impatient though and took me before I was dead. I knew it was too good to be true, but I just wouldn't let myself accept the fact. I was caught up. I . . . I was lost."

"You're dead as far as anyone else knows," Blake said. "We went to your funeral and everything."

"I know, I know," his uncle replied. "It's all part of his plan to make you think . . . Look Blake, I think we're fucked here. Really and truly fucked."

Blake flinched at hearing the word 'fuck' come out of his *actual* uncle's mouth this time. It was jarring and held the weight of not only genuine concern, but terror. The incoming applause was accompanied by music that entangled with sounds of an overenthusiastic audience.

"Uncle Gene . . ."

Blake looked around pleading for his uncle to hurry. If they were entering the final show on the tape this could very well be the last time the two of them could speak uninterrupted, or maybe even at all. He could be marching to his own doom without knowing where he was or why, which was par for the course when it came to everything else in Blake's life. It made sense for the same to apply in his death.

"I know, I know," Uncle Gene barked. "I'm not really dead, Blake, but I might as well be. Mirim lied to you. There's no way for me to get out of this place now. I'm stuck here and you'll be too if you don't get out soon."

"You make it sound like I can just leave whenever I want," Blake fired back.

"I'm sorry," Uncle Gene said. "I know it's not as easy as that, and I didn't mean to make it sound as such. It's just . . . it's more than imperative we figure out how to get you home before . . . before you're stuck just like me."

"Stuck? What happens if we don't find . . . if I do get stuck?" Panic seized Blake, choking out his surging annoyance. "What about the window? I could see into my apartment through the camera lens in the last show, the one Mirim climbed out of. There were some guys in there watching me or us on the television. They could see me and knew I could see them."

"You saw . . . how many were there?"

"Two of them." Blake's words spilled out quickly. "Do you know who they were or what they wanted? Can we get out that way, I mean like through the lens, or window, or whatever it is?"

"I thought so when I first saw the window into my own apartment, but I don't know if it works like that. I never got a chance to try. By the time I found I could look through, they were already making it look like I was . . . they were staging my death. One was dressed like a police officer, the other an EMT."

Blake flashed to the garment bag he saw draped over the armrest of the couch and imagined it contained similar disguises for who he assumed were Mirim's men. He imagined the two strangers laughing as they dressed, drawing straws to see who got the pleasure of notifying his mother of his demise. The two of them delighting over being able to deliver news of a dead loved one to the same woman twice in two weeks.

Blake couldn't let *that* happen to his mother, and he couldn't let *this* happen to him. He still had one last shot to find the window again before the end of the tape, and if he had to dive headfirst into a camera lens to try and get home, he was ready to do so. Maybe he'd be able to pull Uncle

Gene through with him, and the two of them could take care of the jerk-off henchmen in his apartment together.

"We have to try," Blake pleaded. "We have to find the window again."

"I've been hiding in the tape since my first time through." His uncle continued like he wasn't listening about the window, like he'd already written it off as a lost cause. "I couldn't figure out how to leave, but in trying, learned I could hide in shows that had been recorded over and work back and forth through them. It's like separate small pops of reality stacked on top of each other. Once I learned to navigate the cracks, I found I could keep moving."

"That's what yo—*he* told me, the younger you," Blake said. "He said he was moving through the tape too, but could only talk to me in the blank spaces between shows. Like . . . like this. And why are the shows so crazy and violent? The games are different, the people are monsters or mutants. They weren't like this when you recorded them. Does it have something to do with the curse you were talking about?"

Over Blake's shoulder, Uncle Gene watched the incoming lights of the final show approach. They both recognized the theme music from *Family Feud* as it came barreling towards them.

"Mirim's curse keeps him stuck on the tape. I don't know much about where he's from, or what he really is, only there are others like him in positions of power. Like a court or collective, something like that. They're not of our world, not even close. Mirim did something big to piss them off, big enough they imprisoned him on the tape then banished it. Somewhere along the line he ended up on our plane of existence."

Blake's head was spinning from the overload of nonsense he had no choice but to take as fact given his experience thus far. His uncle was talking about curses and creatures from another universe, things that shouldn't make sense but were now frighteningly all too real. He did his best to wrap his mind around what he was being told.

"Like the *Phantom Zone* from Superman?" Blake asked.

In his mind, he could see the pane of glass spinning through space with General Zod and company trapped within a two-dimensional hell known as the *Phantom Zone.*

"I don't know what that is, but if it helps make

the connection, then yes. It's just like the *Phantom Zone* from Superman." Uncle Gene sighed.

"Is he a god or something? Is he an alien or a ghost?"

"Yes," Uncle Gene replied. "He's all of those things depending on who you ask. The short answer is he isn't from around here, and while he may be doomed to the eternal loop of this VHS tape, he's incredibly powerful. He can't leave, *but* somehow figured out how to bring people in and absorb their energy. He thinks he can become strong enough to escape the tape, like it won't be able to contain his power anymore and he'll be free."

"But if he's from a galaxy far, far away or something, how does he have people working for him in our world like the guys in my apartment?"

"The same way any being gets deified and collects followers." Uncle Gene spoke matter of fact like what he said was common knowledge. "The Internet for Christ's sake. Word travels, stories are passed down, seeds are dispersed and planted. Just like Jesus, or Xenu, or Vishnu, or any self-important idiot cult leader finds a flock. It only takes a few weak-minded people to start following something blindly without questioning motives or morals. I'm sure there are countless small sects around the world dedicated to entities we've never heard of."

"Okay, Mirim already has us on the tape. Why doesn't he just zap us or absorb us now and get it over with?"

"I wondered that at first too. I thought maybe it was just a way to toy with me. Draw out the terror, help pass the time," Uncle Gene replied. "It doesn't appear to be the case though. The only caveat he seems bound to is having to let the person go through the entire tape, but you saw how he's been able to get around that. He creates those holes or tears to pull his prey through to the next show and keep advancing them before they have the chance to attempt an escape. I'm surprised you found the window. I used to think I was lucky in that I figured out how to hide, but I'm not sure it's a good thing anymore."

"So, what, you're ready to give up? If he hasn't gotten you yet *and* there's at least one rule Mirim *must* follow, it stands to reason there are more. We just don't know them yet. You figured out how to hide within his prison, a place he should know better than anyone, but here you've been evading him this whole time."

"Yes, but he brought you in to drive me out of hiding and now has us both. Mirim's movement through this place is unrestricted. He can move forward, backwards, and across every layer of information magnetized to the tape on these spools, but it's not that easy for me. I have to *find* the pathways between. Mirim can rip holes or materialize himself from place to place; I have to crawl through hidden slivers of light like a mouse or a roach. I've been moving constantly since I got here trying to stay ahead of him by blending in as contestants or hiding among audience members, and I'm just . . . tired. If this is how my life is going to be forever, I don't want to do it anymore."

"That's why yo—"

"There's no way out, Blake!" Uncle Gene shouted to be heard over the music and applause of *Family Feud* as it encircled them in sound a light. "Not that I know of at least, outside of maybe dying for real, and I don't even know that for sure. I'm sorry he tricked you into this, nephew. I wish I never woul—"

"WAIT!"

His cry cracked like a thunderclap, and everything stopped. Tracking marks froze in place and flickered while the scene materializing around them became a frozen blur of formless colorful blobs. Blake could still move and a quick glance at Uncle Gene told him he could do the same. They both knew what had happened.

Mirim paused the tape.

18

"THE TWO OF YOU ARE AS GOOD AS FUCKED."

The voice of Mirim surrounded them and closed in. The vibration hugged against Blake's body like a static bodysuit, and Uncle Gene bristled as sound waves crashed into him. A squiggly flash of tracking zipped between them and suddenly Mirim was standing there in the form of younger Uncle Gene. Blake stepped back and stood at his real uncle's side to face their shared adversary.

"Well, well, well," Mirim said with a click of his tongue. "If it isn't 'the one who got away'. I've been looking forward to having you stand in front of me once again. And congratulations on the two of you reuniting after a harrowing ordeal. Though I must say, it won't be a lengthy reunion."

"You have to let him finish the tape," Uncle Gene said sternly. "You have me dead to rights, but he still has a chance. He still gets to go through the last show."

"Maybe I do, or maybe I don't." Mirim smiled and began to pace. "Maybe you don't give me enough credit, hmm Gene?"

Uncle Gene's posture stiffened, and he clenched and unclenched his hands trying to downplay how uncomfortable he felt standing in front of a monster disguised as a version of himself. Blake could only imagine the mind fuck.

"I may have to let him finish." Mirim pointed at Blake. "But it's only a formality, and a brief petty one at that. As far as I'm concerned, you're *both* finished."

"Cram it dick-lick."

Blake was surprised at his cocky abrasiveness, and from the look on his face so was Mirim, though the beast recovered quickly from the brazen retort.

"Oh, things will be crammed," Mirim said. "You'll be on the receiving end, I'm afraid. Also, any dick-licking you experience will forever alter the definition in your mind removing any pleasantness to which it may be associated. As I was saying, I will let Blake finish the last show on the tape, and as a bonus rather than snuffing you out immediately, I'll be allowing you to join him, Gene. I've been waiting for this and I'm going to . . . play with you for a while. Both of you. It's not like I don't have the time."

Taken aback, Uncle Gene balked at a response; the words caught in his throat. He wasn't sure how to feel or react. He didn't know if this was a good thing or a prolonging of the inevitable. Seeing the doubt in his eyes and fearing his uncle may give up on the spot, throw in the towel right then and there, Blake spoke up, taking over the conversation.

"Okay then, let's do it," Blake barked. "We accept. We accept . . . whatever you said, just start the show."

"Accept what? Mirim didn't offer us anything. Blake, I don't' thi—"

"Start the show!"

Blake yelled over his uncle's attempted interjection and Mirim, still in Uncle Gene's form, smiled widely. The skin of his face pulled up and back giving more of a snarl quality to the expression, exposing oversized teeth each bearing smiles of their own to create a grotesque kaleidoscopic effect.

Sound and color sprang to life all at once and Mirim disappeared behind a swirling blur of light as the set for *Family Feud* snapped into focus. An extra-wide podium materialized in front of Blake and his uncle springing up just past their waists, while across from them another appeared with their opponents standing behind. Mirim had split himself into five Uncle Genes to take on Blake and his *real* uncle.

Uncle Gene struggled to gain his bearings, saw who they were up against, and knew the reprieve he'd been granted was most definitely *not* a good thing. His nephew may be optimistic, but they were in for a fate worse than death. Despite the cliché, it was true.

There wasn't a doubt in Uncle Gene's mind that ceasing to exist would be far and away better than experiencing a fraction of what Mirim planned to do to them during the snippet of fine family television into which they'd been thrust. Finding a way out would not be easy. Uncle Gene figured the cracks he typically slid through were being watched or already made inaccessible with Mirim having him in his clutches. He'd still keep an eye out.

Uncle Gene hoped if the time came, he could force Blake through while he stayed to accept Mirim's torturous punishment. He was done running, but that didn't mean his nephew couldn't start. Blake was younger after all, had more energy, more stamina. He would be able to hide longer, hopefully long enough to find a way out, long enough to wear Mirim down. Maybe even beat him.

The theme music hit its peak volume, and the swelling sounds of applause from the studio audience nicely accompanied the excitedly upbeat tune. Uncle Gene stared across the stage into five sets of Mirim's eyes, all telegraphing fury.

"Hey everybody, who's ready to play *Family Feud*!"

"Goddamnit." Uncle Gene said, loud enough for Blake to hear.

"What? What is it?" Blake whispered.

"Why did it have to be a Steve Harvey episode?"

19

"WE HAVE A GREAT GAME TODAY between our returning champion family, the Genie-Weenies." Steve Harvey gestured to the name as it lit up on the display behind the five young Uncle Gene's, and the audience erupted in cheers. "And their opponents, the Dick-Licks!"

The crowd simmered with tepid applause as the words 'Dick-Lick' did indeed glow from the display behind Blake and Uncle Gene.

"Great," Uncle Gene huffed. "First, we don't get Richard Dawson and now we're the Dick-Licks."

"What should we do?" Blake turned to his uncle trying to speak in hushed tones. "We can't play the game, right? Or should we?"

"No," Uncle Gene said flatly. "No, we should *not* play the game."

"Hey there Dick-Lick family," Steve Harvey called to them from the center podium. "There'll be plenty of time to chat later. Right now we have a game to play. Send your first player on down and we'll get started."

One of the young Uncle Genes already stood at center stage on his side of the double podium, his hand hovering above the buzzer at the ready. He was smiling with all of his teeth, who were smiling with all of theirs.

"Unfortunately, we need to buy time," Uncle Gene told him. "So, we have to play. At least for a little while."

"Do we even have *that* much time?"

"Dick-Licks, stop dicking around and send up your first player," Harvey barked from the podium. "Time to get this show on the road."

"Stalling won't make this any easier on either of you," one of the other uncles waiting at the podium said.

"If we did, we have less of it now," Uncle Gene said, pushing Blake out toward center stage to man their buzzer. That was when Gene saw an opportunity hiding between the floor and the base of their podium. "Just . . . do your best and follow my lead."

"I don't even know what that means."

Blake whined, stepping slowly across the shiny tile stage afraid it may open up and swallow him at any moment. He looked around as he stepped up to his buzzer, taking in his surroundings. Everything looked just as it appeared when he watched the show on television, at least for the moment. The unsettling toothful smile of the cloned Uncle Gene standing across from him was all that stood out against the familiar set design.

"Thanks for *finally* joining us," Steve Harvey quipped, then mugged to the camera waiting for laughter that came a beat too late. "Blake Dick-Lick, I believe you know your opponents and our reigning champions, the Genie-Weenie family, quite well as I understand."

"I—I'm no—"

"Fantastic," the host interrupted. "Let's see who will take control of the board first with this question."

Blake was panicked and the distorted horror-show of a face across from him only amplified the feeling. He felt like he was going to faint or vomit, or one then the other, in no particular order. He forgot how to speak, how to comprehend words and their meanings when strung together to form a statement or question. A question like the one he was supposed to be listening to, but for the life of him couldn't tune in for.

He remembered his uncle's words and focused on them. *Do your best. Follow my lead.* The lines became a mantra that anchored him back to the bizarre reality of which he'd become a part, and if he wanted to get back home, he'd need to trust his uncle. He would need to do his best. Suddenly, Blake could hear *and* understand what Steve Harvey was saying. He was back in it.

"*We* asked one hundred people the same question and put the top five answers in order on the board."

Blake stared down the freakish face of Mirim's twisted version of his uncle, no longer intimidated by its terrifying appearance. He snuck a quick glance over his shoulder hoping to lock eyes with Uncle Gene and nonverbally communicate how he would not let him down, but he was gone. There was no one behind the Dick-Lick family podium. The settling calmness shattered as panic took hold of Blake once again until a glint from one of the camera lenses caught his eye. He'd almost forgotten about the window.

A high-pitched squeal sounded from somewhere above, cutting off the host and prompting all five members of the Genie-Weenie family to cover their ears. Blake thought he was having a panic attack again until he saw Steve Harvey looking around screaming for someone to 'make it stop'. Then, suddenly it did and was replaced by a booming familiar voice.

"We asked a hundred people a question," said the voice. "And they unanimously said for you to FUCK OFF!"

"What?" Steve Harvey stumbled back, looking around for who the voice belonged to. "That's not even a questi—"

A shiny tip pushed out from the front of Harvey's chest and the remainder of the blade quickly followed, plunging to his groin. The confused Harvey tried to turn around when the sword was withdrawn, but a pile of his insides slipped out from the hole in him like mud down a mountainside. They hit the tile floor with the wet slap of fresh sliced ham on a clean glass tabletop.

The viscera spread out from beneath in all directions polluting the shiny tile like oil gushing from the ruptured tanker of a doomed ghost ship.

Harvey toppled forward face down into his own insides, and the swordsman stepped up slinging blood from his weapon before sliding it into the scabbard slung across his back. The assassin was none other than Richard Dawson himself. Not the original host of *Family Feud*, but easily the most recognizable and prolific. Known as much for his charm as his sometimes-questionable regular practice of kissing *every* female contestant on the lips.

Blake stepped away from the puddle of mangled guts and blood spreading from the eviscerated Steve Harvey, wary of what the conquering Dawson would do next. He assumed this was Mirim's doing; him toying with them, working to ramp them up through non-stop gratuitously violent vignettes, allowing them to burn on the brink of madness for a bit before smothering them into oblivion.

Across from him, the five young Uncle Genes looked just as confused and scared as Blake, which made little sense and added to his increasing unease. Blake turned to run toward the audience away from potential death-by-disembowelment and ran smack into Uncle Gene.

"What the . . . what the hell?" Blake mustered, collecting himself from the sudden start.

"Pretty cool, huh?"

Uncle Gene gestured as Richard Dawson gave several swift kicks to the side of his slain adversary, each impact sending spouts of blood spraying into the air.

"Did you do that? Was . . . was that you?" Blake motioned to the disturbing scene.

"Turns out there was an old Dawson *Family Feud* episode on this tape. I remembered passing through it quickly at some point but hadn't been able to spend any time there yet. I guess you were right about Mirim having to follow other rules too. Like not being able to be in two places at once.

"He was focusing so much on this place, *this* game, he forgot to pay attention. It was easy to slip away without him noticing once I saw a crack. I pulled Richard Dawson back here with me after a quick stop at an old samurai movie I found buried under two episodes of *Mr. Belvedere*. Doesn't really take much to rile the old guy up. Dawson was more than willing to come help us out."

"He's *helping* us?"

Blake saw the five young Uncle Genes had all turned their focus on him and his uncle, ignoring the carnage-fueled siege transpiring at the host podium. They knew they'd been duped, and they weren't pleased. Five terrifyingly unique visibly etched versions of exaggerated rage sieged their faces, turning the once identical Genie-Weenie family into a varied band of anger-fueled ghouls.

Behind them was Richard Dawson donning a powder-blue suit with matching patent leather shoes. The ensemble was unfortunately spattered in blood and body fluid, which had been unavoidable, but he handled it with aplomb. Dawson ran his fingers through his hair, and the blood holding it back in place added to his quaffed psychopath look.

His smile was unrelentingly bright, a high-watt halogen beacon that projected confidence, but most importantly, the smile was normal. It was the right size for his face, and the teeth hadn't been replaced by something sinister, or given teeth of their own. It remained uncorrupted by the bizarre, unmolested by horror, and was the most beautiful thing Blake realized he'd seen since long before being trapped on a VHS tape.

"Do you think this will stop me?" All five Genie-Weenies hissed in unison. "You're both as good as dead."

A buzzer went off like a chainsaw cutting through sheet metal. The Genie-Weenie standing at the podium didn't realize Dawson had pulled his samurai sword again until it was already buried in his brain. The conquering host had brought the blade down with smooth precision into the top of his head, splitting his skull open down to his nose. The crimson spray was a dazzling eruption of ruby-colored liquid sparkles that would've been whimsical and joy-inducing under different circumstances.

"I'm afraid that answer didn't make the board."

Richard Dawson flashed his winning smile and ripped the sword up and out of the bloody gorge he'd gouged into the Genie-Weenie's head. Glimmering, thick, wet drops leapt from the blade, forced off from its momentum, formed a glistening arc of red across the stage. The mortally wounded Genie-Weenie twitched amidst the already weakening blood flow from his head, and his eyes went crossed. His lower jaw hung loose like he was going to say something, but instead his tongue unfurled, convulsing like an electrified garden slug.

The Uncle Gene creature began to teeter and would've fallen on his own in a matter of moments if Dawson hadn't planted his size eleven, light blue, patent leather oxford between his shoulder blades. The kick was delivered with a tremendous amount of force behind it, sending the evil clone to the floor face-first and in a hurry.

Blake was in the unfortunate position of having an unobstructed view of his opponent's nose colliding with the tile, followed by the crunch of shattered bone being pushed up into his face. The impact forced the wound in his head open farther, spouting sticky bits of swollen brain matter across the floor like wet pink and gray confetti. A co-mingling of fluids pooled around the vibrating body of the fallen Genie-Weenie as confused nerve endings fired signals to receptors that didn't know how to receive them, or just plain didn't exist anymore.

The other four appendages of Mirim, the remaining Uncle Genes, climbed the podium stalking toward Blake and his uncle. Their teeth, now elongated and drawn to points, were void of their own tiny mouths. Their eyes had gone large, round, and black. Not shiny, but matte. The optical orbs not only reflected no light, but actively deflected it making the sockets in their faces seem impossibly dark and empty.

"The window," Blake said, pointing at the audience and crew. "I think I saw the window out there. We have to go check."

The podium collapsed and crashed forward under the weight of the dissected Mirim, as the creatures writhed in various states of drastic transformations. The flesh of the four uncles undulated as their bodies twisted and swelled into a hideous amalgam of horror. They screeched and shrieked as bile and strands of thick sticky fluid dripped from their orifices, while their bodies thrashed in pain-filled metamorphosis.

"Pucker up you ugly bastard fucks." Richard Dawson stepped up brandishing his sword, assuming a fighting stance. "I've got enough goodnight kisses for all of you . . . Oh shit!"

The host leapt back as the body of the creature whose skull he'd just bifurcated began to grow and change as well. It lifted its head and sneered up at him through the rearranged features of his flat and busted face. Its skin bubbled and moved like a pot of boiling rubber, and two hands reached out of the opening in its head pushing the wound apart wider. There was a crackling wet tear as something attempted to escape the husk.

"Go," Uncle Gene said to Blake, pointing back toward the cameras. "Find the window and try to get through. I'll stay here with Dawson and hold off Mirim."

"What? No." Blake pulled his uncle's arm. "Let the sword wielding psycho deal with it himself. He seems to be doing fine so far."

"No, Blake." Uncle Gene ripped his arm from Blake's grasp. "I'm already stuck here, and I told you I'm tired of running. If you can't get out through the window, you have to hide. Find the cracks and slip through like I did. Maybe you'll be able to figure out how to beat Mirim at his own game. Maybe you can actually go home someday."

"But Mirim could be lying," Blake cried. "We don't know wha—"

"Exactly," Uncle Gene raised his voice over the chaos closing in. "We *don't* know. We don't know anything, which is why you *have* to keep going. You need to see if there's really a way out of . . . this. Now please just . . . just go."

A gurgled shriek erupted from the mess of monsters approaching Dawson at center stage, as a thin, moist, pink-skinned creature slid from the hole in the downed Genie-Weenie's head. It slapped the tile followed by a gush of brownish red slime covering the thing. Blake's uncle gave him one last look before turning to stand against the fray with Richard Dawson. He saw in his eyes there was no changing the man's mind, so Blake turned from the impending brawl toward the cameras.

20

EVERYTHING IN FRONT OF BLAKE was dark. He thought maybe the audience and crew had vanished but realized his eyes were adjusting to the sudden lack of light as the camera's silhouette came into view. It wasn't the right camera though, not the one in which he thought he'd seen the window, so he quickly changed course, veering left.

From behind him came a monstrous bellow followed by a tremendous crash as part of the set collapsed, but Blake didn't let himself turn around. He was afraid of what he'd see, but more so afraid of what he'd do, or wouldn't do. If he turned and saw his uncle in peril, he didn't know if he'd have the courage to help fight. If he didn't see it, he wouldn't know, wouldn't have to think about it, at least for now.

The crew and cameramen stood slack-face and still, like cardboard statues. They were perfectly still, having no reaction to what was happening on stage. Even the audience was strangely silent, absorbing the unfolding carnage from under the cover of darkness. Blake briefly wondered if they were all hollow husks, 3-D printed from the mind of Mirim, to fill space in his own private Phantom Zone, or if any of them had once been actual people before their life-force was sucked into the void of a cruel being's insatiable appetite.

He had no idea how long this had been going on, after all. It was possible every person he'd seen or come in contact with on the tape was once on the outside. One moment they're living their life like normal, the next they're stuck on a videotape, with no idea why or how, only to end up a mindless and malleable toy. A catch-all stand-in for the wiles of a tantrum throwing deity, lashing out at disciplinarians who are most likely unaware of and/or apathetic to his efforts.

Blake nearly tripped over a bundle of cables and snapped back to his task at hand. If those were real people at some point, he felt sorry for them but had no time for pity. He refused to let himself become one of them. Now within ten feet of the camera there was no doubt he'd found the window. He saw a scene playing out in the lens as he approached like it was a tiny television screen. The camera operator didn't so much as flinch when Blake put his face against the lens.

His hopes fell when he saw it wasn't his apartment he was looking into until he realized it *was* his apartment, and dread consumed him. The two men he'd seen earlier in the jumpsuits were still there but had now changed clothes with one wearing a police uniform and the other dressed as an EMT just like his uncle said. The garment bag draped, empty and limp over the back of the couch.

The reason the apartment seemed foreign at first was due to its current state. The two intruders, the men of Mirim, were trashing the hell out of his place. The one dressed as an EMT slashed the couch cushions with a box cutter, while the faux policeman used a crowbar to bash holes in the drywall of the living room.

"Hey!" Blake screamed into the lens and banged the glass with his fist. "Stop!"

He didn't know what else to say, but it worked. For a moment, at least. The EMT heard him first and paused mid-slice to look around for the source quickly realizing it was coming from the television. He smiled and waved to the police officer who was bashing another hole in the living room wall. The fake officer looked up, his expression signaling he wasn't happy about being interrupted mid-destruction until he realized what his partner was trying to tell him. Then he was all smiles.

He walked around the couch to join his friend obviously chuckling, as they pointed despite there being no sound. Their mouths moved as the two had a short verbal exchange, and Blake tried in vain to read their lips. It wasn't as easy as it seemed when actors did it in movies or on television shows. Blake couldn't even tell if they were speaking English. He imagined the two men in his apartment speaking to each other in French and laughing in loud and obnoxious stilted chortles.

"I didn't say you could slip me the tongue, you rat-bastard!"

Richard Dawson growled from behind him, followed by another crash, and this time Blake couldn't help but look. The five other uncles, formerly known as the Genie-Weenie family, were separate entities no more, having now fused together into the sole being of Mirim. The hulking creature was much bigger than when they'd encountered it on *Supermarket Sweep* though just as hideous.

A tumescent tongue like a prehistoric anaconda extended from the mouth-hole while the rest of Mirim's face churned to form his abhorrent visage. The constrictor-like tongue had wrapped around Richard Dawson's waist, yanking him from the floor toward the beast's salivating maw. Blake looked back over his shoulder just in time to see the sword-wielding host slice through the thick corded muscle of the organ and drop back to the ground. Mirim howled as Dawson wrestled to remove the severed tongue from around his waist and get to his feet.

The entire studio filled with the hot stench of spoiled meat and sun-bloated fish as Mirim expelled an unholy wail. Blake's eyes scanned the stage for his uncle but found no sign of him. Quickly, he turned back to the camera lens, the window into his apartment, a portal through his television screen by way of magic provided from an antiquated piece of forty-year-old technology, and found the police officer and EMT had moved in closer. Their smiling faces filled the small space with vicious half-sneers of crooked teeth tinted yellow. Blake pounded against the lens yelling, and then he started punching.

The glass didn't so much as smear from his attempt to assault his way through, and he looked around desperately for something to break it with.

"How do I get through?" Blake leaned to the side, calling to the camera operator across from him. "What do I need to do? Smash it? Burn it? Is there some spell I need to say first? Hello? Can you hear me?"

He couldn't though. Every member of the crew remained motionless, non-playable characters suspended in time; placeholder pieces used as set dressing. He grabbed the camera from both sides and tried to tip it over, but it wouldn't budge. His palms stung with vibration from slapping uselessly at the large device. The men were doubled over laughing harder now, and the EMT put his hand on the police officer's shoulder saying something to him.

The phony officer nodded and wiped the back of his hand across his face as his laughter tapered. He said something back to his partner pointing first at him then the television screen. The man dressed as an EMT nodded and pointed at the television as well, using his other hand to remove the remote control from his back pocket.

Panic raced up the back of Blake's throat, constricting his airway as he pounded on the lens and the side of the camera, screaming. His hands and fingers ached, his arms burned, but the lens refused to give under the force of his blows. He couldn't stop. He had to get through the window. Blake had to go home.

The two men smiled wide and gave half-hearted sarcastic waves with wiggling fingers. The EMT pointed the remote at the screen, pushed the power button, and he and his partner disappeared, leaving only an empty lens. The television was off. The window was closed.

Blake's screech was cut short by shredded, overworked vocal cords. He collapsed to the ground.

21

IF THERE'D BEEN ANY OTHER WAY for Blake to see into his apartment, he'd be watching the police officer rip the flat-screen television from the mounting bracket, yank out any connecting cables, and leave it against the wall in the hallway. It would remain there until they were through wrecking his place and ready to leave. Then they'd take it with them.

Blake was on his knees in front of the camera, his back to the stage. The battle between man and beast raging behind him sounded like it was getting farther away as he drifted into shock over the sudden permanence of his new reality. The muscles in his arms went slack, and darkness crept from the edges of his vision blinding his periphery. His chin rested on his chest as he folded forward into himself but was suddenly yanked backwards just before kissing the tile.

"Come on, kid." Blake recognized his Uncle Gene's voice. "We don't have much time."

Hearing his uncle snapped him back from the brink of mental collapse as he realized he was being dragged by the back of his shirt in the direction of the audience. When they reached the bleachers, Blake stood and hugged his uncle.

"Okay, okay." Uncle Gene pushed him away. "I said we didn't have much time."

"Survey says . . . .arrwwghh! Aw, hell."

Blake and his uncle turned and watched Richard Dawson strike out with his sword unsuccessfully at the writhing serpentine arms rushing toward him. In a single motion, so quick and fluid, the efficiency of movement was impressive enough to almost distract from the grisly result. Mirim grabbed Dawson around the chest with one disgustingly strong appendage and around his ankles with the other, lifted him in the air, and ripped the man in half as if he were made of soggy paper.

Blood, intestines, and smuggler's smorgasbord of organs spilled out like yolk from a broken egg adding additional spattering to the organs already left by Harvey on the floor. The creature tossed the two halves of the great Richard Dawson away and turned its sights on Blake and Uncle Gene. The upper half of the discarded host landed in front of them with a wet smack. His tongue lolled from his mouth, and his eyes were rolling around in their sockets. The samurai sword remained clutched in his hand, and the tip tapped rhythmically against the floor as misfiring nerves sent spams up and down his arm.

A victorious roar erupted from Mirim, vibrating the air throughout the studio. A swarm of tracking lines raced across the ceiling to gather around the creature's head as if waiting for the command to attack. Uncle Gene grabbed Blake by the arm and pulled him around to the back of the bleachers. The crowd remained unreactive, silent. They were shadow people existing in more than two dimensions, but not quite three. The ground shook and Blake stumbled, catching his balance on one of the support beams pulling his uncle to a stop.

"Wait," Blake coughed. "The window . . . it's gone. What . . . where are we going now?"

"You have to hide." Uncle Gene was stern and loud. "Now shut up and follow me."

Tracking lines tore through the bleachers sending ripped fragments of lumber and cardboard people into the air like they'd gone through a wood chipper. Uncle Gene pulled Blake forcing him to follow before the floor could be cut out from under them again. His uncle had somehow found him after they'd fallen into darkness from *Supermarket Sweep*, but if it happened again that wouldn't be the case.

Blake and his uncle both knew this was it. This was the end of the tape, and there was nowhere left to fall, no more room to play with. The game was over, and Mirim was ready to declare victory and collect the spoils. A two-for-one deal comprised of uncle and nephew. The one who got away, and the bait used to draw him out. The creature was on the verge of relishing in his winnings, but Uncle Gene had other plans.

The set was being shredded and whittled away by roaming bands of razor tracking lines slicing madly as the energy around Blake and his uncle took on a charged and frenzied feel. The heated incisions sent sizzling pieces of ceiling and lights crashing down around them with Uncle Gene yanking Blake out of the way just in time. A growing chasm opened down the center of the bleachers and burst apart revealing Mirim rumbling with fury. The bellow he released polluted the air with another burst of putrid rot rushing from the writhing trash pit that lurked within the creature.

Uncle Gene tugged his nephew over to a camera yet to be compromised in the melee then pulled him to the floor behind it. He pointed at a sliver glow coming from a seam in the ground where the camera met the tile. It was a little more than an inch wide and no more than a foot long, maybe only ten inches.

"This," Uncle Gene said. "This is one of the cracks I told you about. These are what you slip through to hide back in the tape and buy time until you figure out how to beat Mirim and get out for good."

"You mean us." Blake was unable to disguise his panicked desperation. "Both of us. *We're* going to hide until *we* find a way to beat Mirim and get home. Right?"

Uncle Gene grimaced, bit his lower lip, and shook his head.

"Sorry kid. It's my fault you got sucked into this mess, and if I stay with you, I only make things worse. Mirim wants me badly enough to make sure he finds me again and faster this time, which puts you right back in the line of fire. If he's already got me, it'll be easier for you to keep hidden longer. Hopefully, you can figure out this mess better than I could."

They felt the approaching buzz of tracking lines converge overhead as Uncle Gene pushed back against his nephew's pleas to stay together. They crouched in the shadow of Mirim as the thing loomed closer, towering over them while belching putrid smelling howls as he approached.

"How does this thing even work?"

Blake examined what his uncle referred to as a 'crack', confused how he was to fit through. He assumed it was a hole with the rest of it being beneath the camera, but he hadn't had any luck in moving them. He put his hands against the base to push, but his uncle stopped him.

"Just dive into it!" Uncle Gene yelled to be heard over the rising chaos.

"What?"

"I said, just dive int—"

His uncle was pulled back and up into the air like he'd been attached to a rubber band that snapped back. Blake watched Uncle Gene dangle from Mirim's tentacle-like, undulating arm as the beast erupted in peals of terrifying baritone laughter.

"Go!" Uncle Gene screamed. "Now!"

Blake cried out in frustration looking from his uncle to the glowing crack and back again. Finally, he closed his eyes, held his breath, and tipped forward headfirst, hoping he was doing it right.

"Fuck!"

He felt a cold rush of air followed by a flash of light bright enough to see through his closed eyelids followed immediately by silent darkness.

22

Blake found himself alone in the fuzzy darkness for the first time since he'd arrived on the videotape. He could see a square of light up ahead and ran toward it trying not to think about a monster ripping his uncle's limbs off. He couldn't let himself believe Uncle Gene was dead, not again. He didn't see it happen, so as far as he was concerned there was still a chance his uncle was alive somewhere on the tape.

He hoped his uncle had changed his mind about hiding and managed to escape Mirim by sliding through one of the cracks. Blake continued toward the light having already decided he wasn't going to look for a way to escape until he found him. If Uncle Gene did get away it would only be a matter of time before the two of them ran into each other on one of the shows. Then, they'd both leave together.

Blake was within twenty feet of the square of light when he realized what he was looking at. Grainy blurred images became just clear enough for him to see people standing around a swirling disc of color. A wheel. It was an episode of *Wheel of Fortune*, only something was off about the way it looked. Gone were the horror-show smiles, snake arms, and creepy contestants. There were no weapons or acts of violence affixed to the wheel, only dollar amounts and special prizes with glittery backgrounds that sparkled in the stage lights.

Everything about what he was watching appeared normal except the way he was seeing it because the picture was reversed. Like he was standing behind a screen on which it was being projected. Uncle Gene told him he'd hid by slipping through the tape by way of what had been recorded over, and before he knew who Mirim was, other Uncle Gene had told him the same thing. Now it clicked.

Blake realized he was in that place they both described. He was between recordings; the shows stacked on one another from being recorded over. He turned around and looked back the way he'd come, and sure enough far in the distance he could make out another square of light. He looked all around then and could see more of the same in all directions. These were the shows on the tape, and there were a lot more than he'd anticipated. Then again, he imagined most of them were Mirim's perverted versions of the originals populated with vile facsimiles of hosts and contestants designed to torture those unlucky enough to get sucked into his interdimensional prison.

Until Blake could be shown otherwise, he'd be operating under the belief his uncle was still alive, and whether there were ten or ten thousand shows to navigate, Blake was determined to trek through them all for as long as it took to find Uncle Gene again.

He turned back to his view of the spinning wheel of color as it slowed to a stop. Blake took a deep breath.

"This is as good a place to start as any," Blake said to himself. "I'm a *wheel watcher*!"

With that, he stepped through the glowing square and disappeared through the light. He hadn't noticed the swarm of tracking lines closing in behind him.

23

TO SAY BLAKE'S MOTHER HAD BEEN on a bender the past three weeks since he died would be an understatement. She'd been in full-blown, drink yourself to death, self-destruct mode. She'd only just lost her brother and days later her only son was gone as well. The call of his death came during a brief moment of lucidity between vodka and wine-induced mini-comas.

She remembered the police officer identifying themselves and thought she was experiencing déjà vu until he said Blake's name. She had him repeat himself several times asking if he was sure it wasn't her brother Gene he was talking about. Sadly, it was not. She fell so deep into the bottle after that phone call she was out of commission for days until a police officer came to her apartment to check on her. Maybe it was the same one at the scene of her brother's death, but she'd drank that memory away.

She'd been sitting alone in her kitchen staring into a sea of empty liquor bottles splayed across the tabletop when the officer walked on in. She didn't recall hearing a knock and hadn't heard the door open or close yet here was a policeman standing in her kitchen. She'd been so taken aback she didn't ask how he'd gotten in.

The officer told her he was sorry for the intrusion, but they'd been trying to get in touch with her for days regarding her son, the mention of which rocked her nearly as hard as the day she learned he'd died. It made sense since she'd destroyed her phones and been too heavily impaired to notice someone knocking. She briefly searched the booze-addled corners of her liquor-soaked mind for the memory of exactly how he'd died but couldn't quite shine a light on the thought.

She thought maybe she remembered something about a heart attack, but Blake was far too young for that unless it was drug-induced. If so, it was something she couldn't bring herself to face and decided she must've buried the cause beneath gallons of her liquid coping mechanism. She wasn't paying close attention to what the officer was telling her until she heard the word 'funeral', after which she asked him to repeat himself.

The officer told her for the second time that Blake had made arrangements for his own funeral previous to his death, something Blake must've decided to do after the passing of his uncle, to not burden loved ones with the task, and she'd missed it. The services had taken place three days prior, and she'd been unreachable despite what the officer claimed were 'countless' attempts to contact her. She'd missed her own son's funeral and upon learning so would've begun chugging herself back into oblivion if the 'police officer' wasn't standing in front of her. As it was, she didn't realize she'd forgotten to breathe for almost a minute.

The officer offered his condolences and gave Blake's mother the key to his apartment saying the landlord was giving her another week to get what she wanted, and the rest was going in the trash. He placed the key amidst the bottles in front of her, apologized again for her loss, and let himself out.

She'd already chugged a third of vodka before the door closed behind him.

She'd only lost two days when she regained consciousness this time and managed to strike enough of a balance with her demons to function long enough to go to Blake's apartment. She wasn't sure what of his she'd take if anything, but she knew she owed it to him and herself to at least go look at what she had left to remember her son by.

She started by taking the bus but got off a stop later, finding that the motion of the metal behemoth made her nauseous, so she took a cab the rest of the way. Her hand shook so violently when trying to insert the key into Blake's door, she had to use the other to hold it steady. She realized upon entering she hadn't been inside Blake's apartment enough to remember much of what it was like. Outside of the handful of times she'd been by when he first moved in, Blake always came to her place for family functions or to visit.

It was a small apartment; she remembered that much, but something bad had clearly happened within the tiny space. Holes of all sizes dotted the walls from the hall into the living room and beyond. Dust from broken drywall layered nearly every flat surface while larger chunks lay splayed across the floor like breadcrumbs marking a path to destruction. There were tufts of white cotton and mangled hunks of yellow foam all over the living room, fragments from what was left of the sofa.

The cushions had been gouged and sliced apart, and the insides hacked to bits and flung all over. The police officer had said nothing about a break-in or foul play, or had he? Either a critical piece of information regarding her son's death had not been relayed to her, or she'd truly firebombed the memory through her consumption of mind-combusting fluids.

She made her way through the remainder of the small floor plan finding more of the same. The bedroom was a wreck, the mattress and comforter having been equally sliced and diced as the couch, leaving feathers covering the floor like a blanket of fresh snow. In the kitchen, every drawer had been pulled out with its contents in a pile on the floor next to where it had fallen.

All the cabinets were open and empty, their insides having been spilled, ripped apart, and busted, covering the linoleum in broken dishes, spilled cereal, and a heavy dusting of flour with baking powder. The bathroom door was closed, and though she could hear water running inside, she didn't bother to look. Making her way back to the living room, she felt empty and alone. Her brother was dead, and now her son was dead. There was nothing left to remember him by because it had all been destroyed.

She scanned the area one final time, intent on leaving as soon as possible until she noticed something. The television was missing from the wall in the living room. There were wires hanging from where it had been mounted, a ring of dust was left in its place, the remote control was on the floor next to the toppled coffee table, but the television itself was gone. On the stand beneath where it had hung sat her VCR, the one Blake borrowed the last time she'd seen him. Sitting on top of the VCR was a videotape and another remote, only this one was partially melted.

She recognized the tape as one her late brother used to record his favorite game shows, as well as the ones on which he appeared. She remembered all the time Blake spent with his uncle parked in front of the television watching the same ones over and over. She snatched the videotape and remote and stuffed them into her purse before tucking the VCR beneath her arm.

She headed for the door kicking drywall and dust leaving a cloud in her wake. It may take her a while to work up to it, but she would honor the memory of her brother and son by sitting down and watching the videotape. If she couldn't be with them anymore, watching the shows that brought her brother and son together would be the next best thing.

She hooked the VCR up to her own T.V. upon arriving home, slid the tape in, but did not push play. She would eventually, but not today. Once her grief had crested and she'd swam most of her way back to shore she'd be able to. Until then, the tape would wait in the machine until she was ready.

-end-

ABOUT THE AUTHOR

JOHN WAYNE COMUNALE LIVES IN THE NEON-DRENCHED CITY OF SIN LAS VEGAS TO PREPARE HIMSELF FOR THE HEAT IN HELL. HE IS THE AUTHOR OF DEATH PACTS AND LEFT-HAND PATHS, THE CADILLAC MAN, SINKHOLE, THE CYCLE AND MORE. HE HOSTS THE WEEKLY STORYTELLING PODCAST JOHN WAYNE LIED TO YOU AND FRONTS THE PUNK ROCK DISASTER JOHNWAYNEISDEAD. HE CURRENTLY TRAVELS AROUND THE COUNTRY GIVING TRULY UNIQUE AND MOST EXCELLENT PERFORMANCES OF THE WRITTEN WORD.

FIND EVERYTHING JOHN WAYNE AT
JOHNWAYNEISDEAD.COM